AF266828

Jesus's Daddie
'Issues, by Joe
OVELMAN, in this
the year of oUR
2025 © Joe OVELMAN

FoR Peace.
FoR moM & PoP. FoR
C, & D, & P. FoR
GMO & GMG. & GDG) & GDO!

Our Stor

a basic pose

event that le

hero with an

child. Two,

y begins with
idon Medusa
aves our
unexpected
actually.

"I'll take it!"

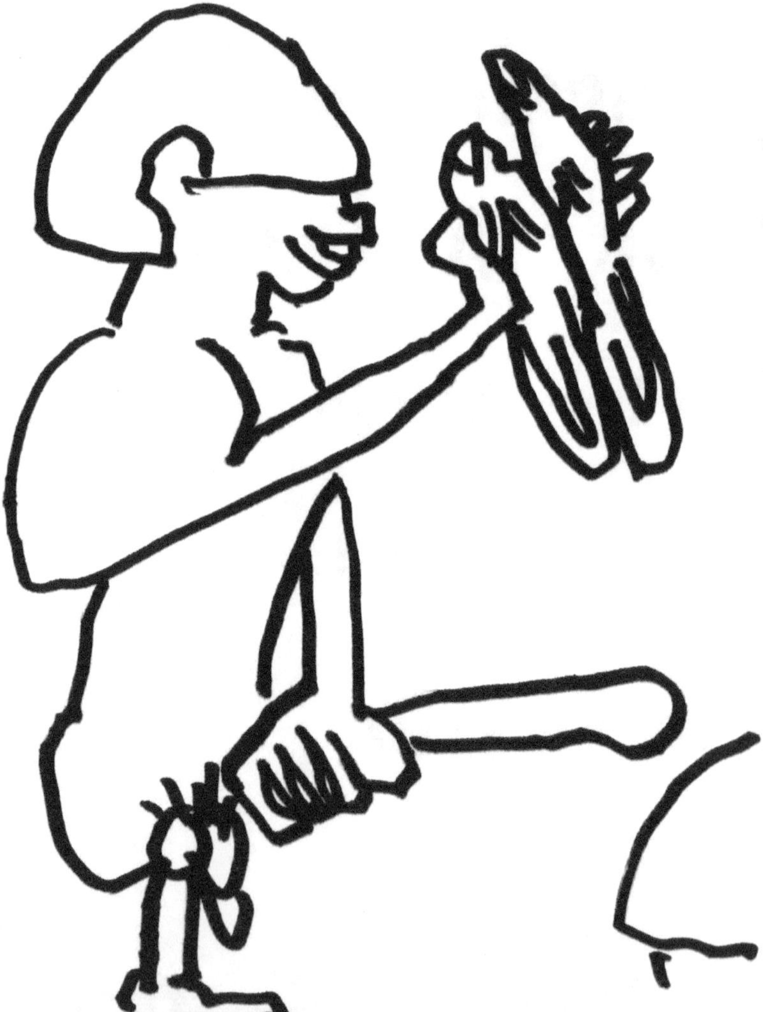

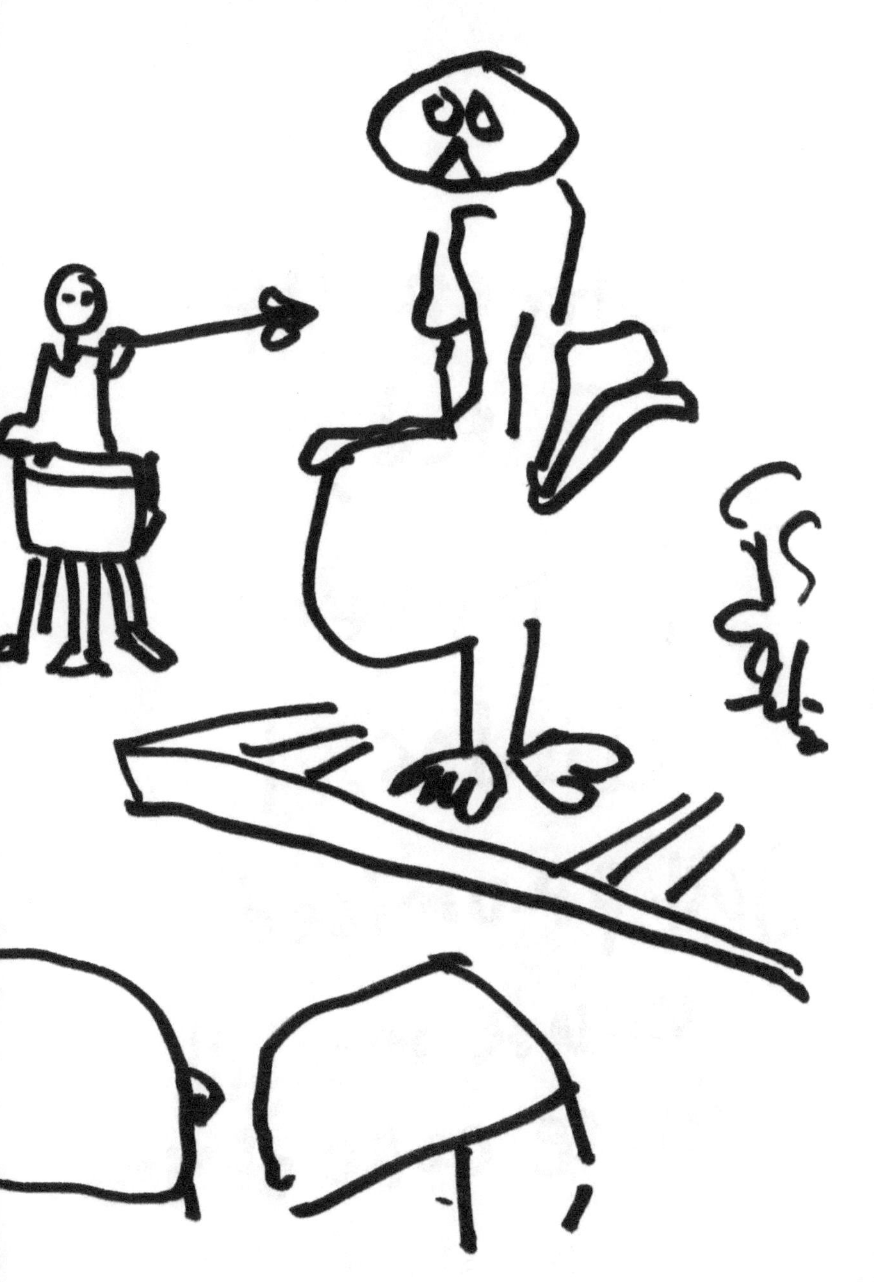

Cheer up,
Bird,
I prefer
dudes. I
just promised
your ma i'd
take care of you.

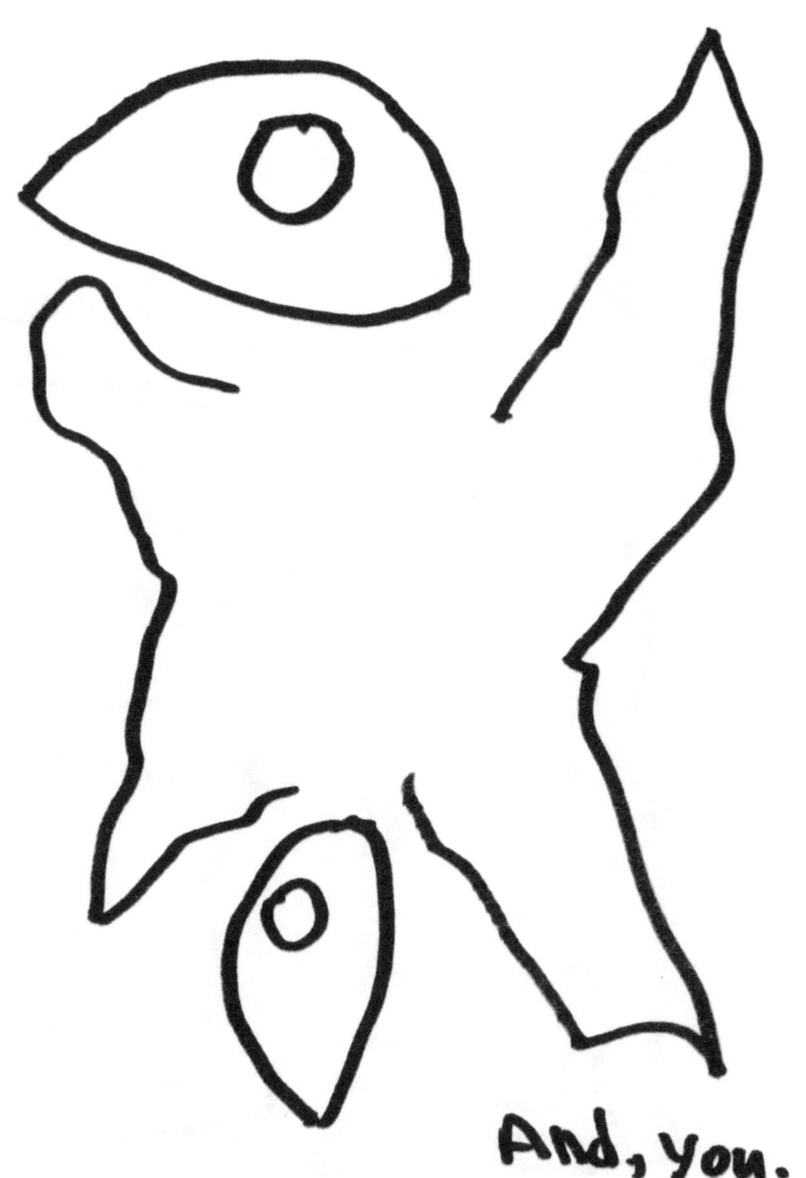
And, you.

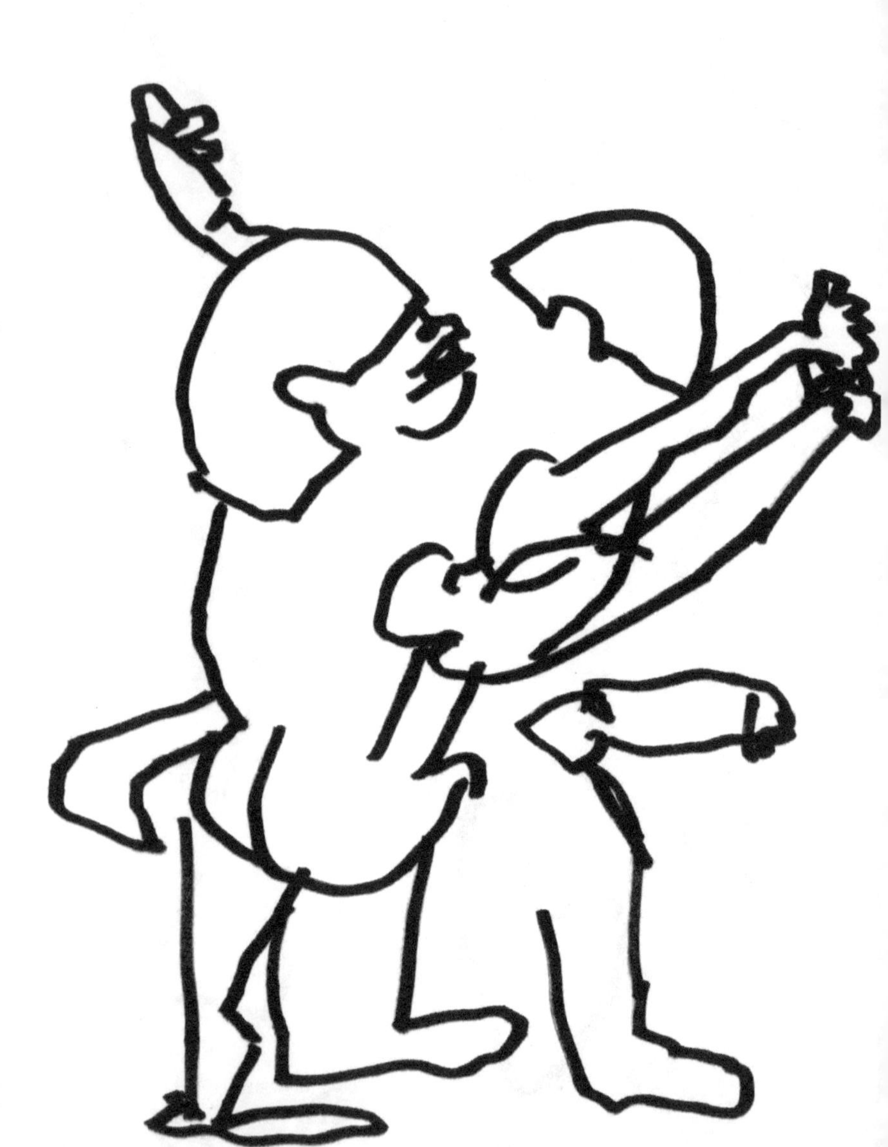

They'll
be at
the market
for at
least another
hour.

Damn.Good.

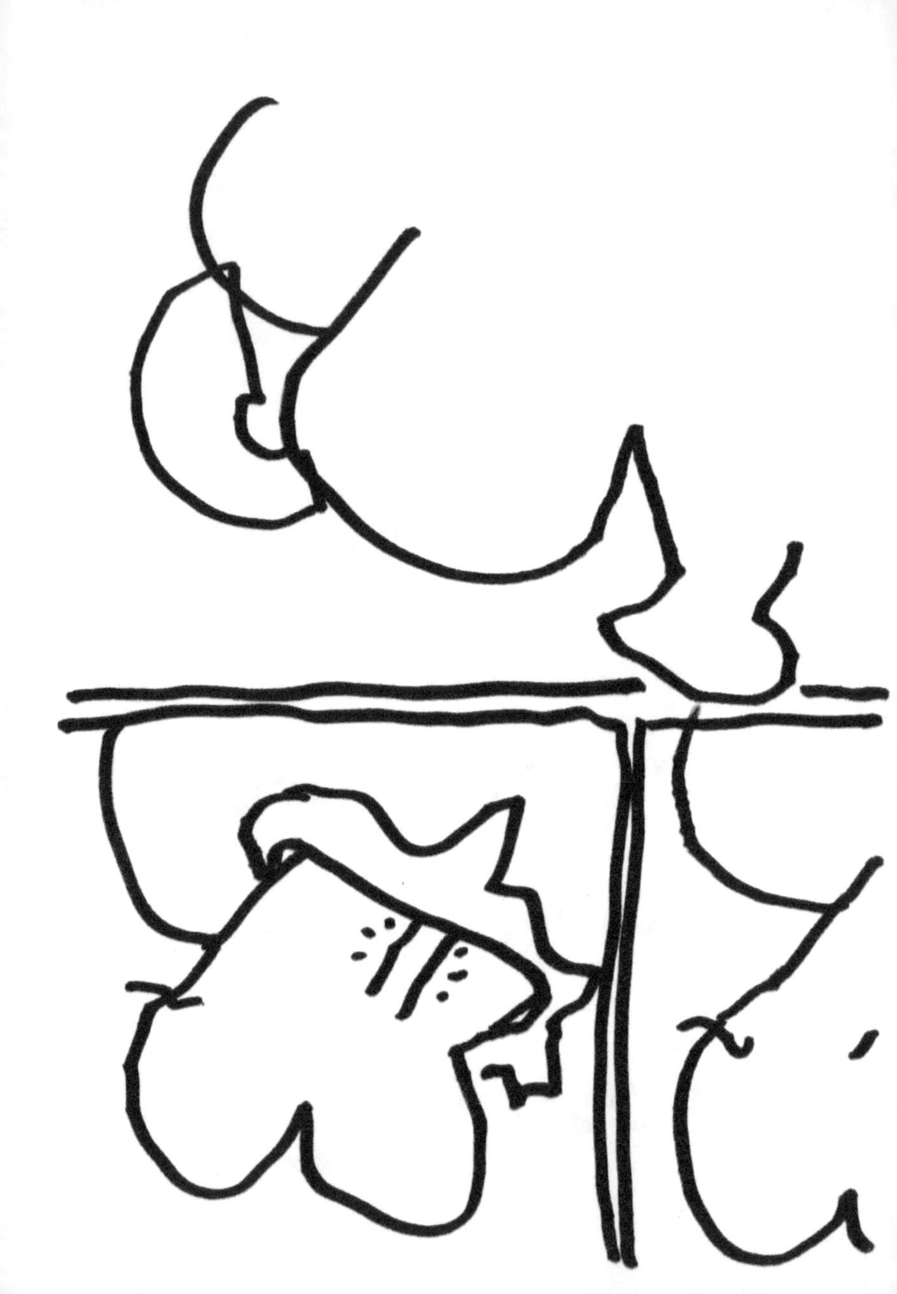

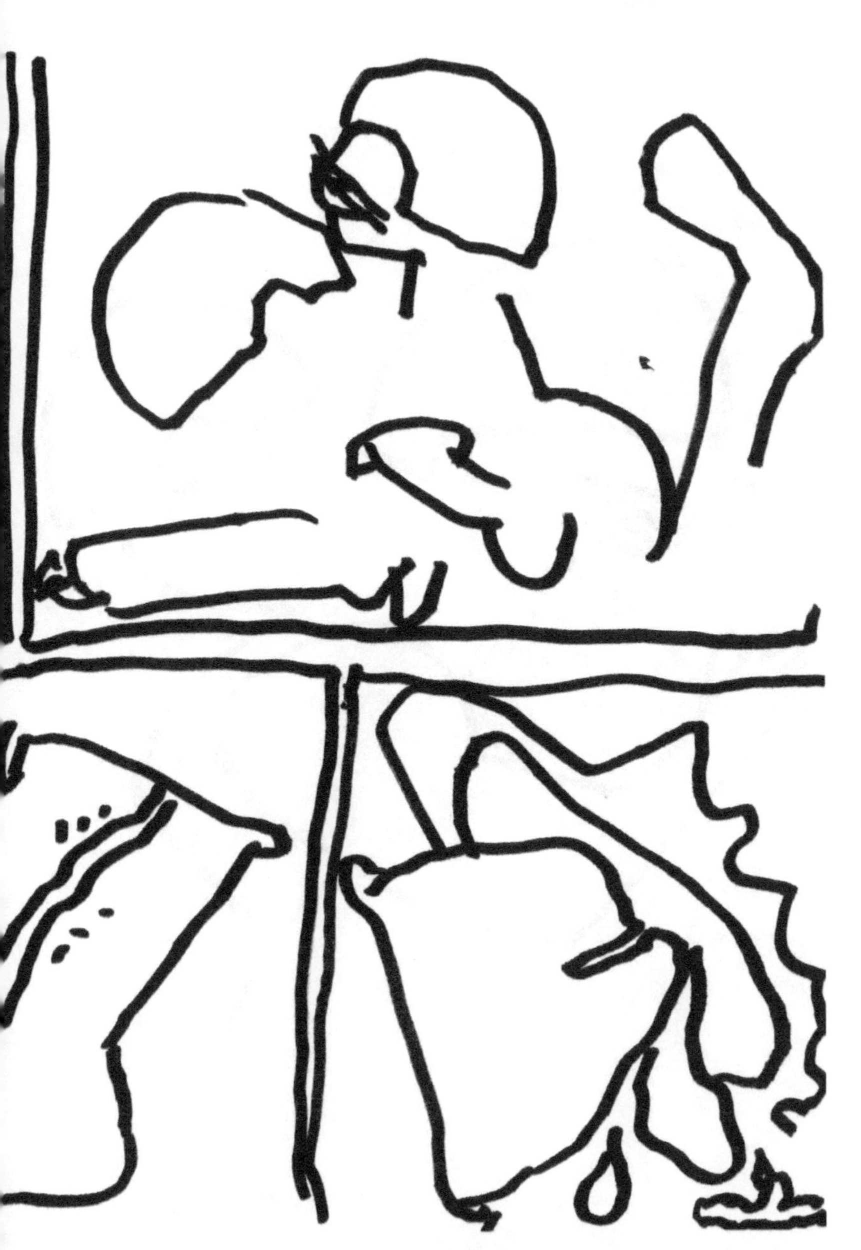

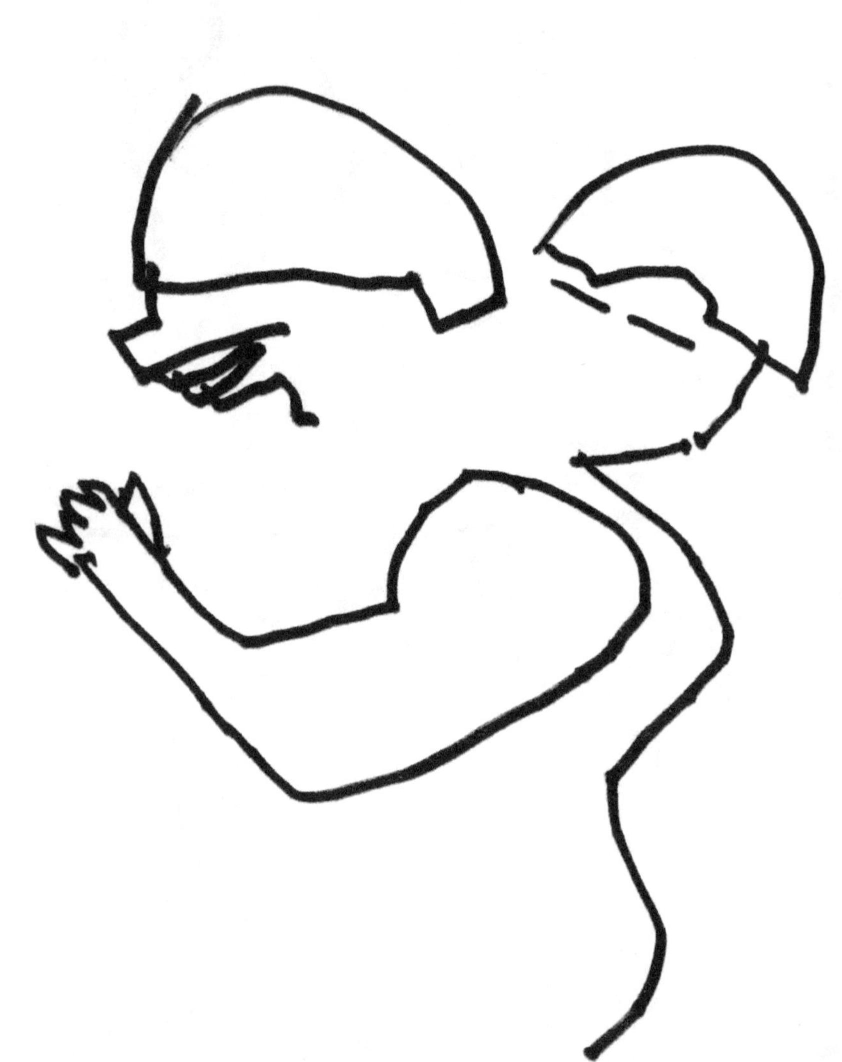

Thanks,
Daddy

Anytime,

(please.)

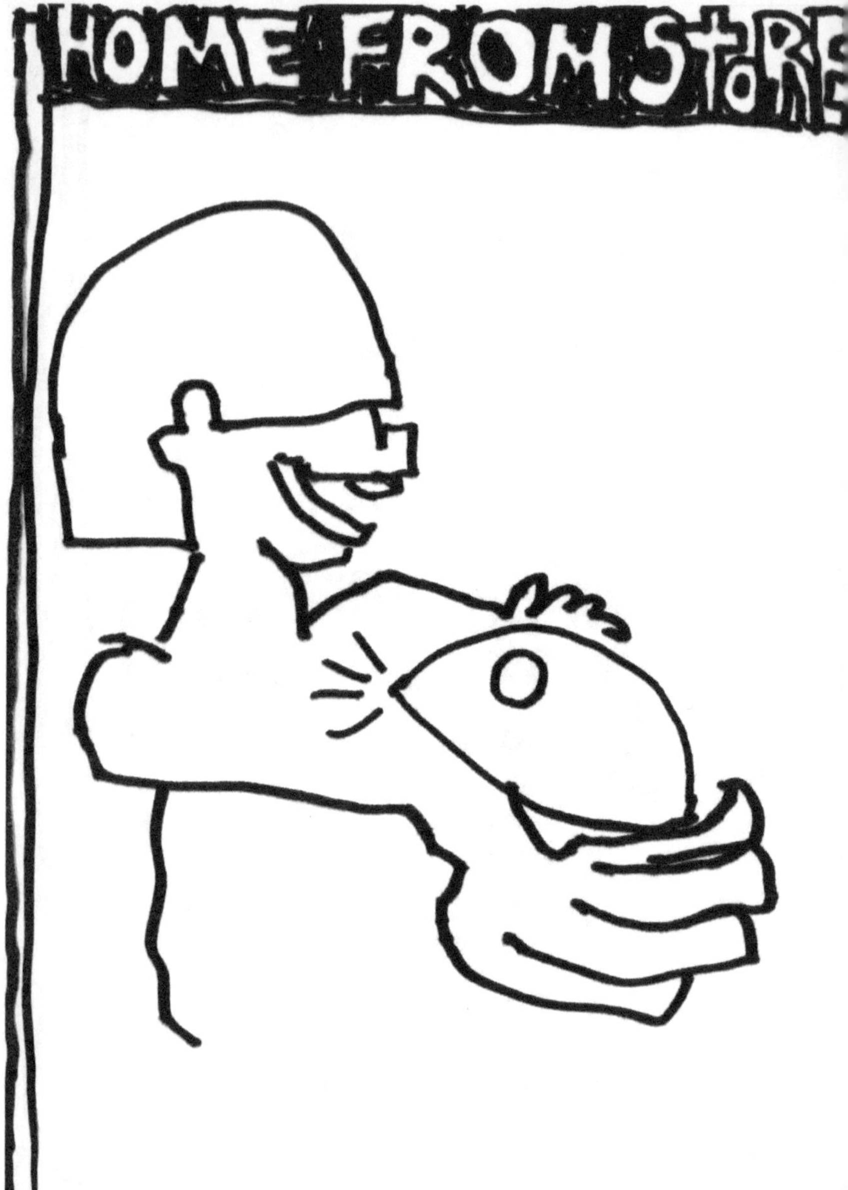

HOME FROM STORE

Papa?

Aaah, hell no, I'm your rich gay uncle, Joseph of Pennsylvania. I like to swim, read, play and reject theism.

I bought
you and
your mother
at an
auction.

(see p. 4) [teen]

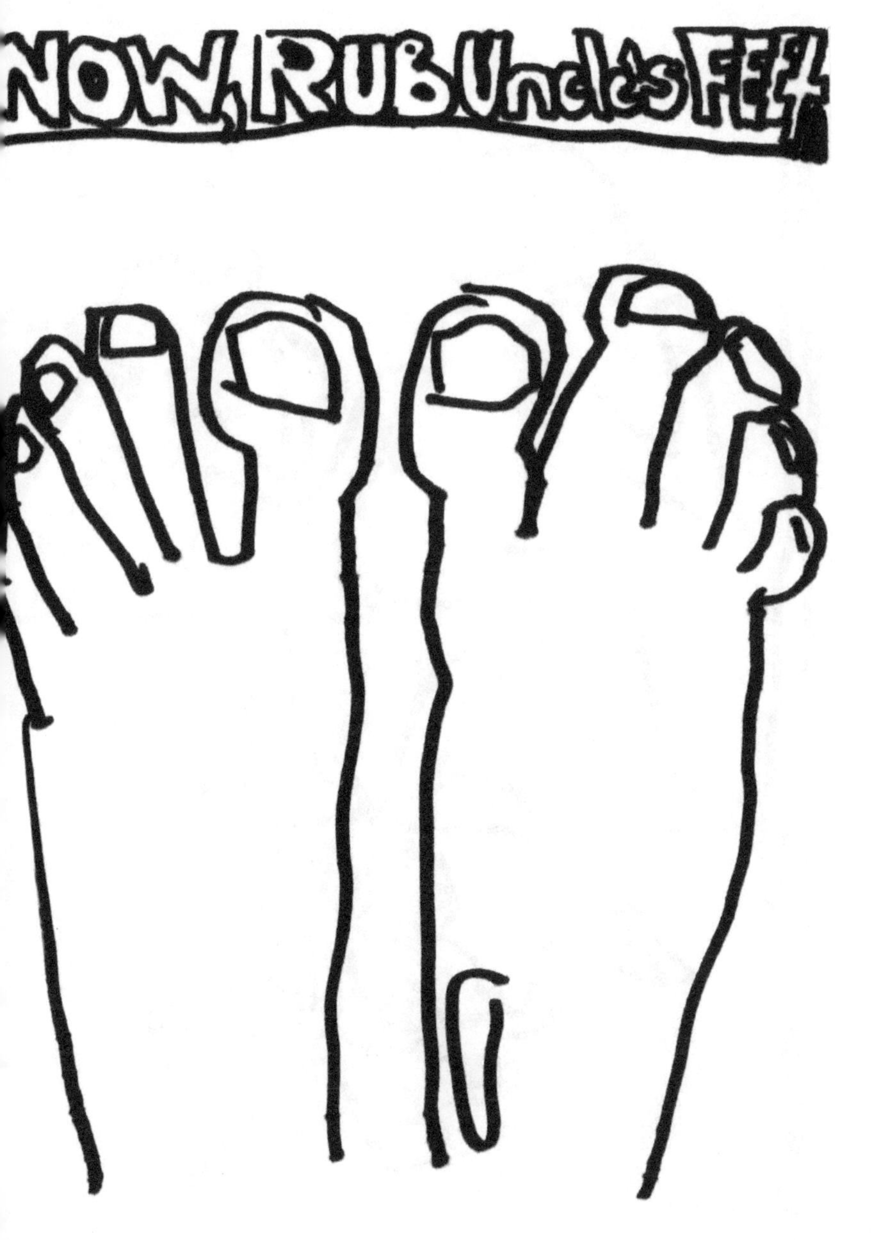
NOW, RUB Uncle's FEET

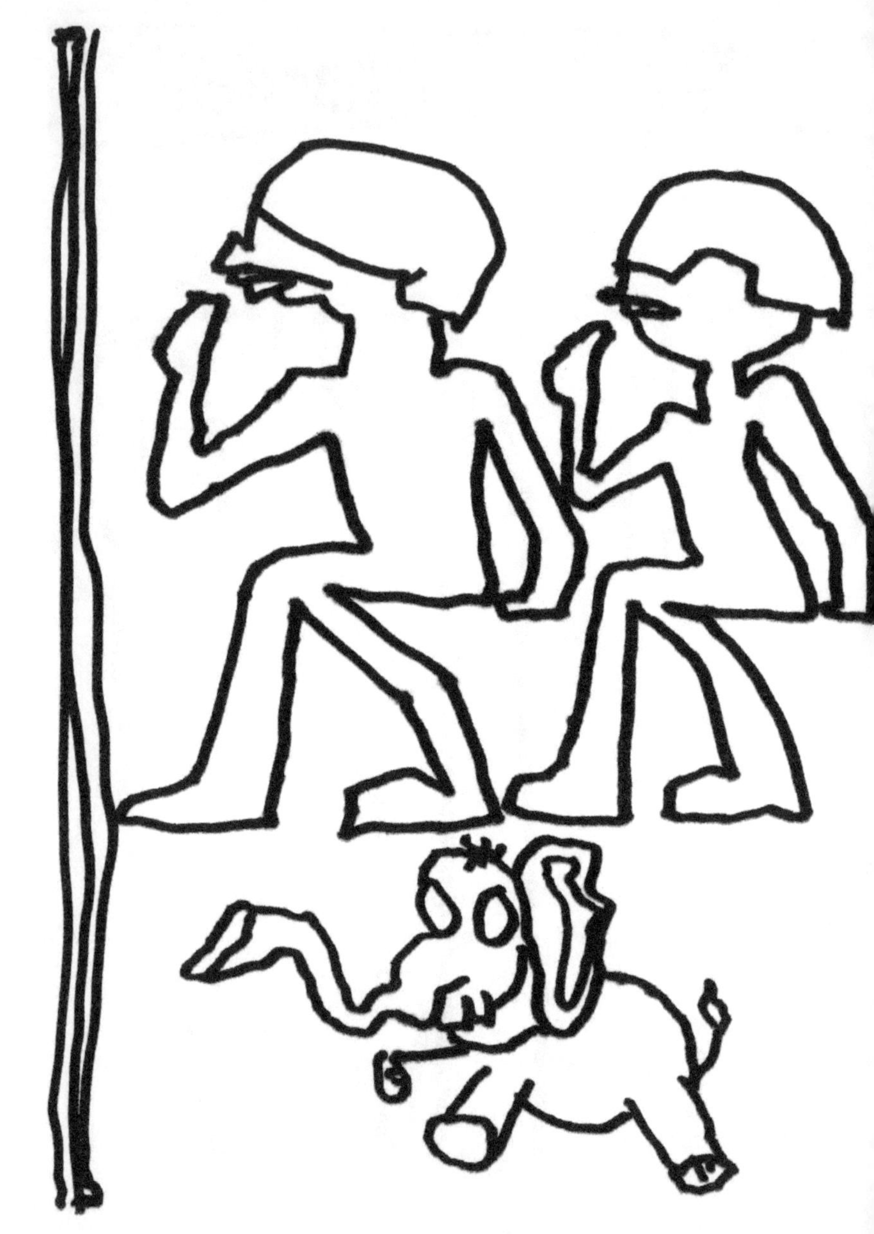

Joseph of
Pennsylvania
told the
infant
stories.

4 yr Old: No, honest,
J.O.P I did not
steal that
pink elephant
from your house
on our play
date.

Also 4 yr old:
J.O.P

walking backwards

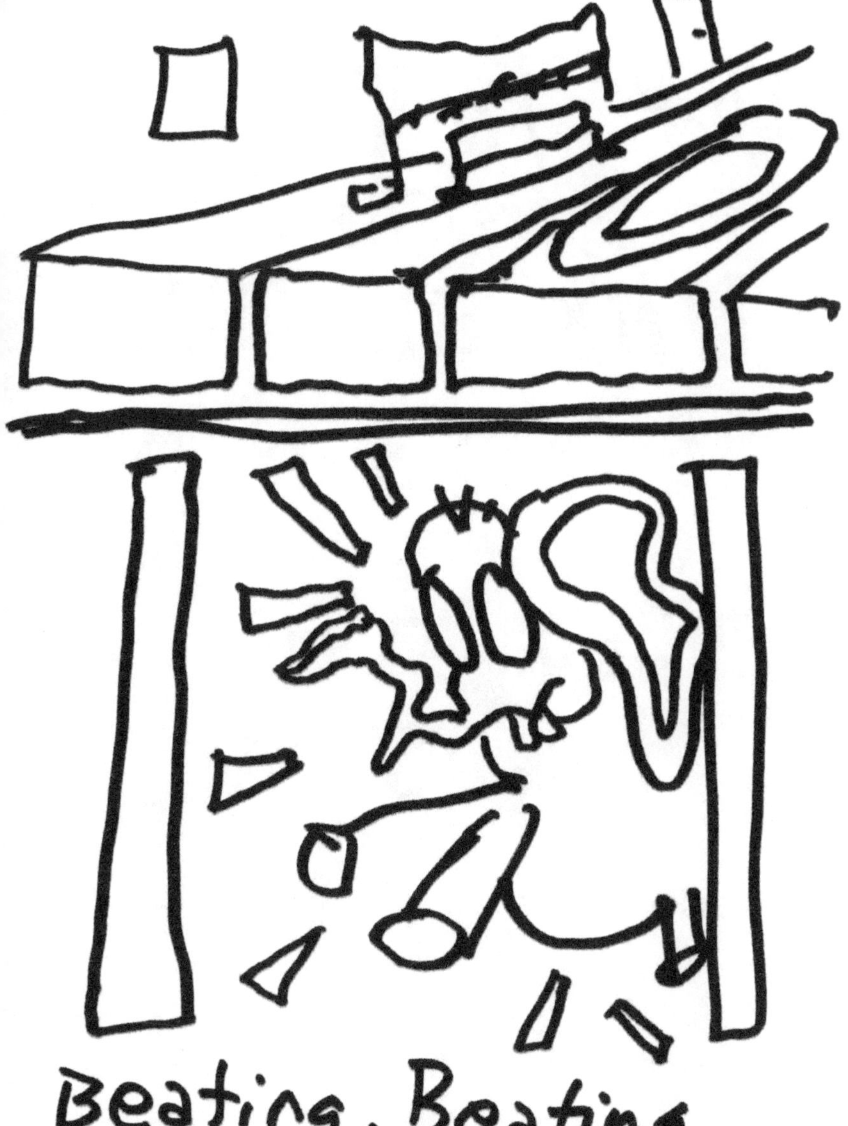

Beating, Beating . . .

J.O.P.: TO THIS
DAY THAT
PINK ELEPHANT
BEATS, INFANT!

Thou shalt
not STEAL.

Also J.O.P.:

Go now and
plow the field.

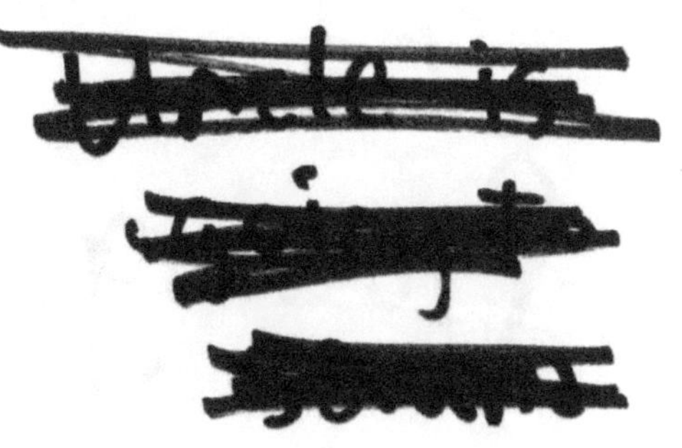

Speaking
of
Plowing...

(Afternoons are
for Saunas,
After All.)

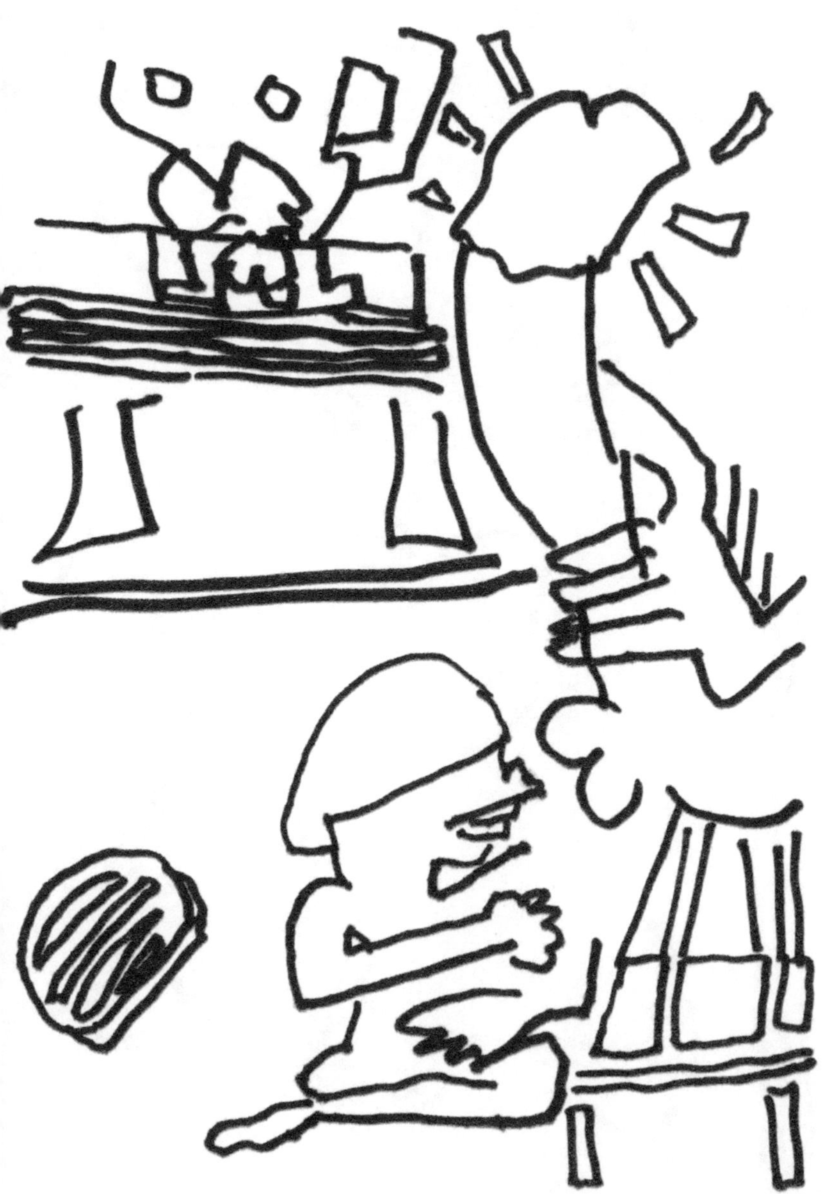

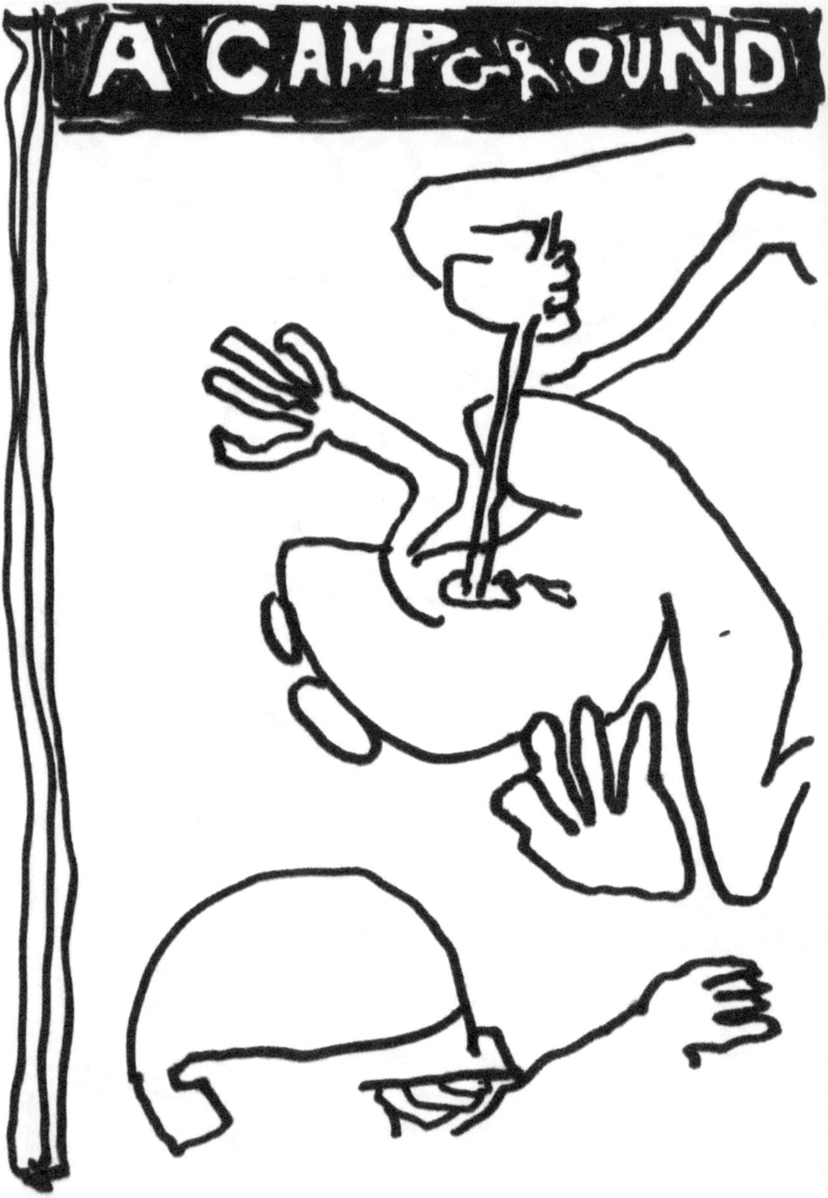

A CAMPGROUND

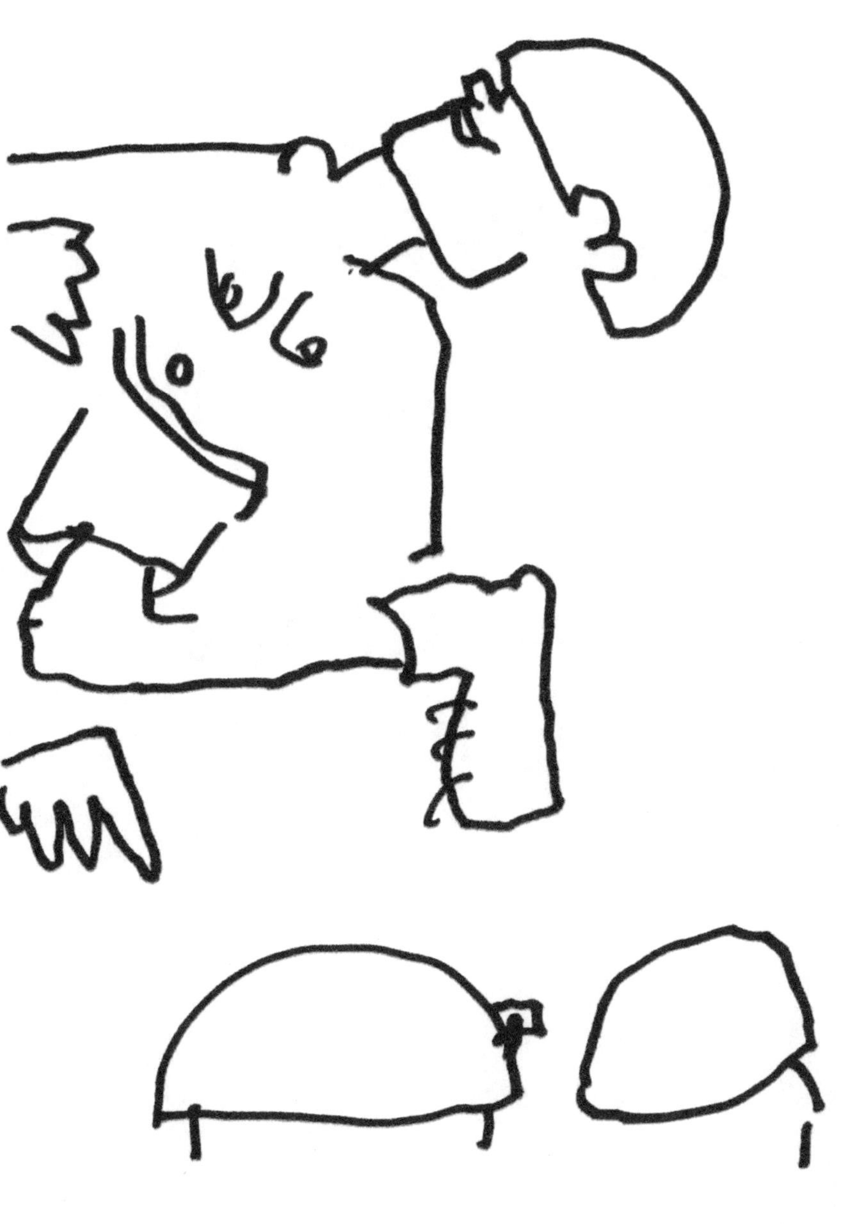

5 YR Old's just
  J.O.P
watched as the
boy tortured and

murdered the
frog. He watched
with a few other
boys.

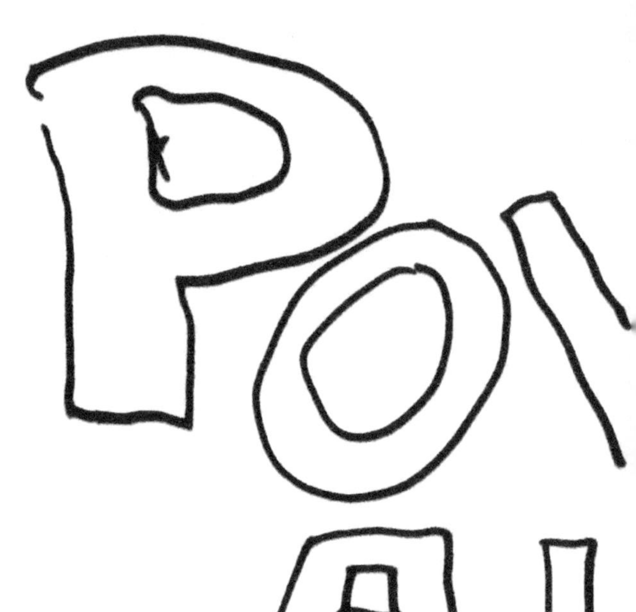

this message b
POW
A I
(where power decid

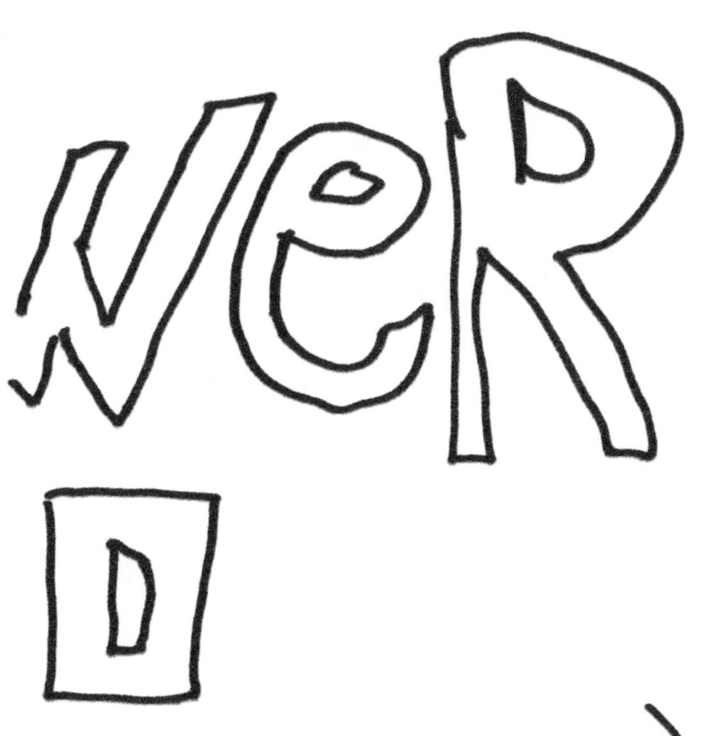
Rought to You by:
NeRD
D
es who gets aid)

thou shalt not kill

CHAPTE8 VERS 17
The 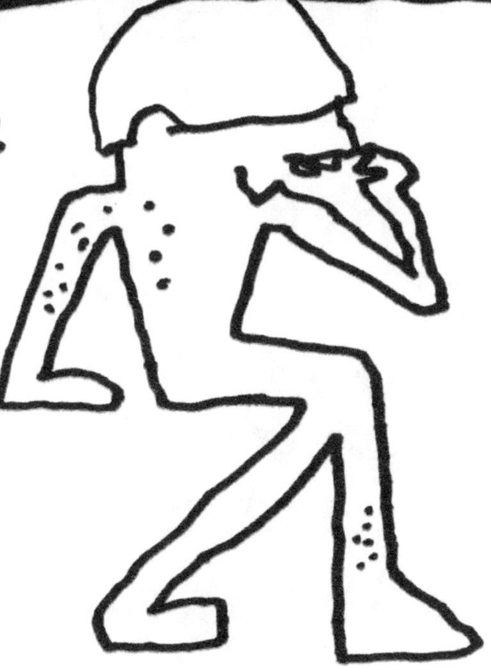
on the

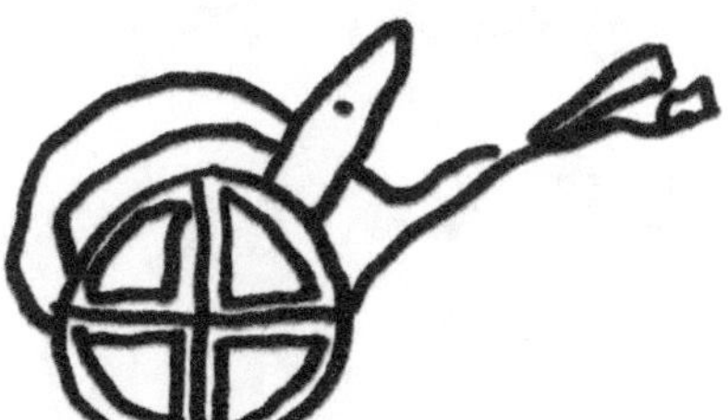

The boy on
the bus
Had a Rash.
We EVERYDAY,
all point
ted and
laughed.
I've never since
allowed myself to
be so cRass [OR
so weak]

Do unto
others
and all that.

I'm really

Sorry,
Dude.

(Circa 1976)

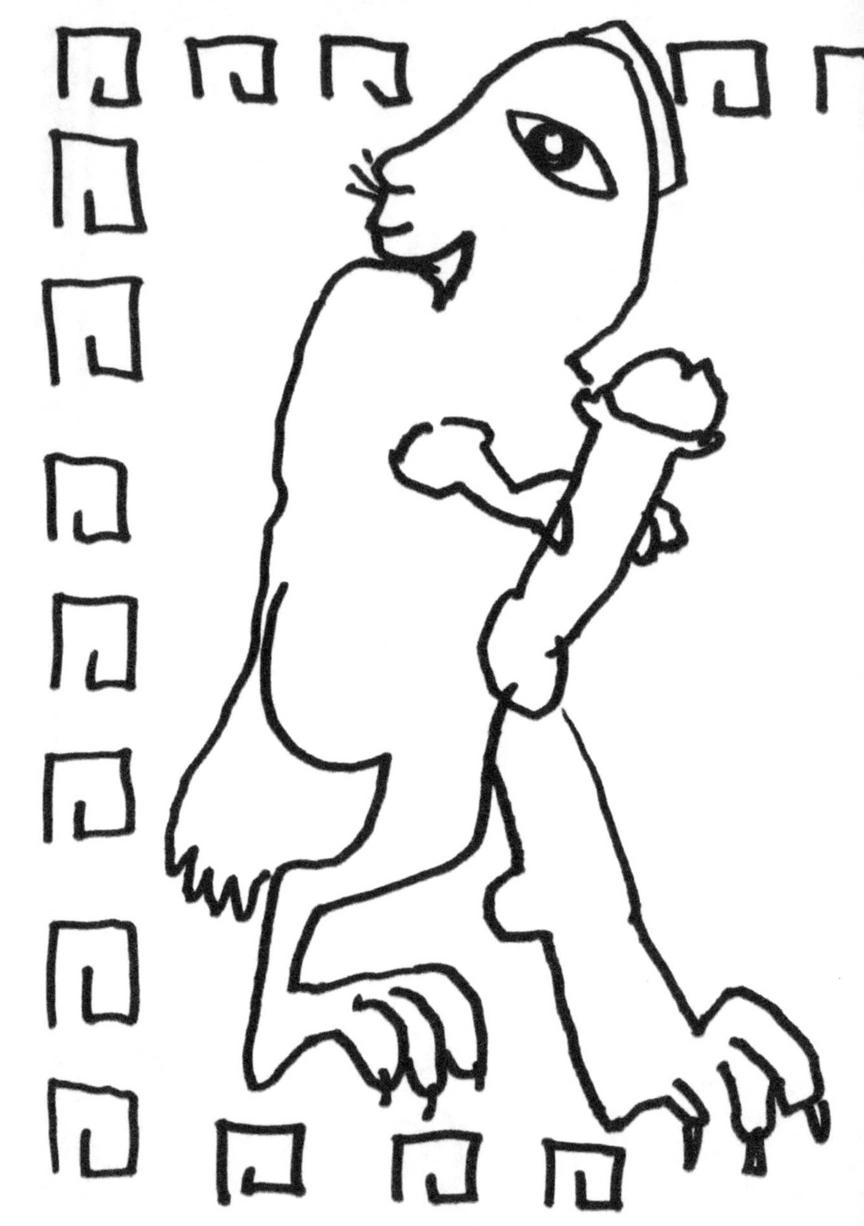

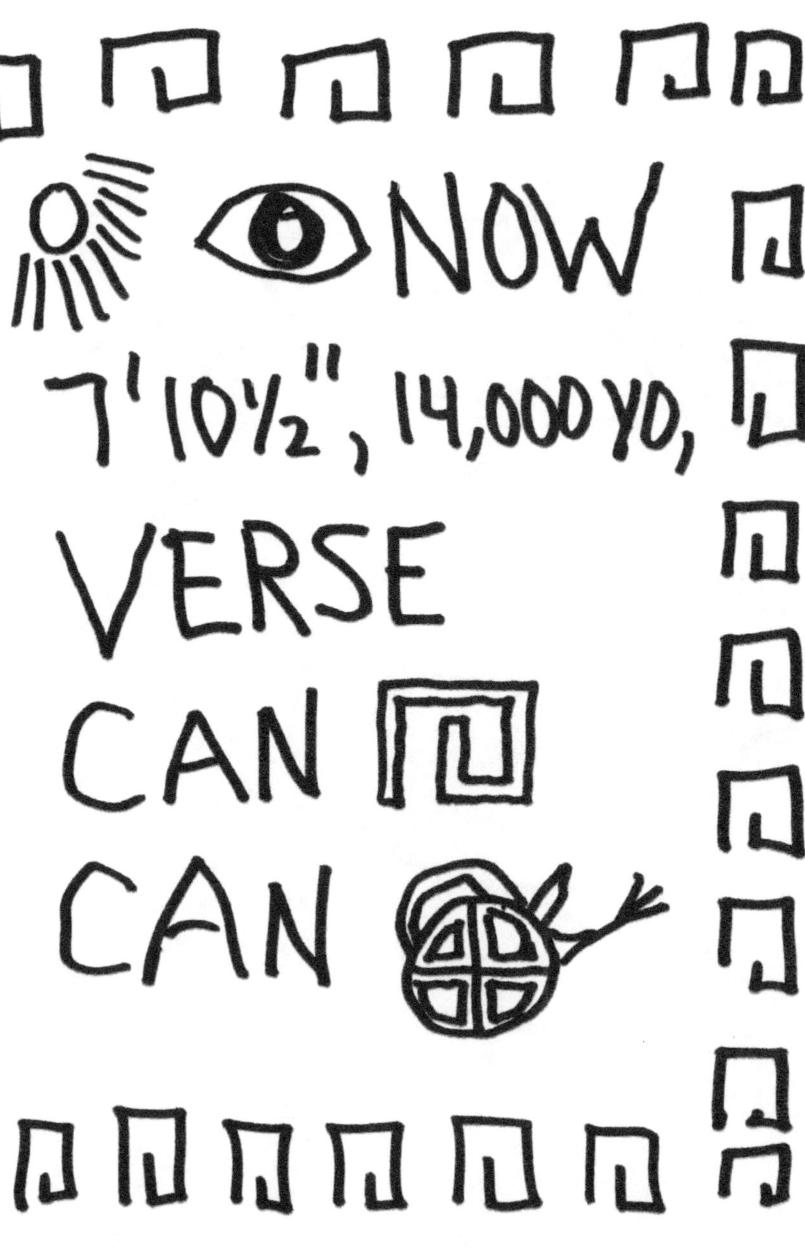
NOW
7' 10½", 14,000 YO,
VERSE
CAN
CAN

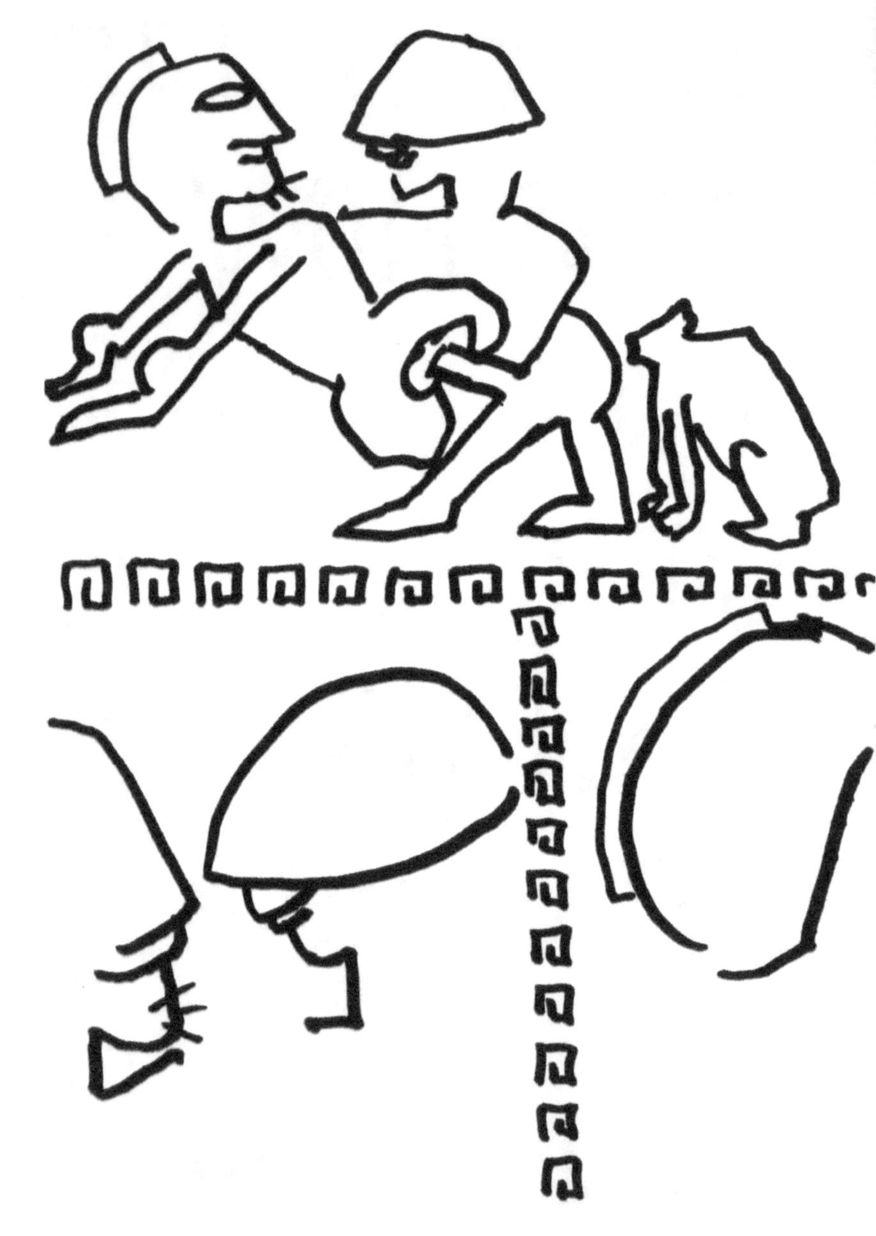

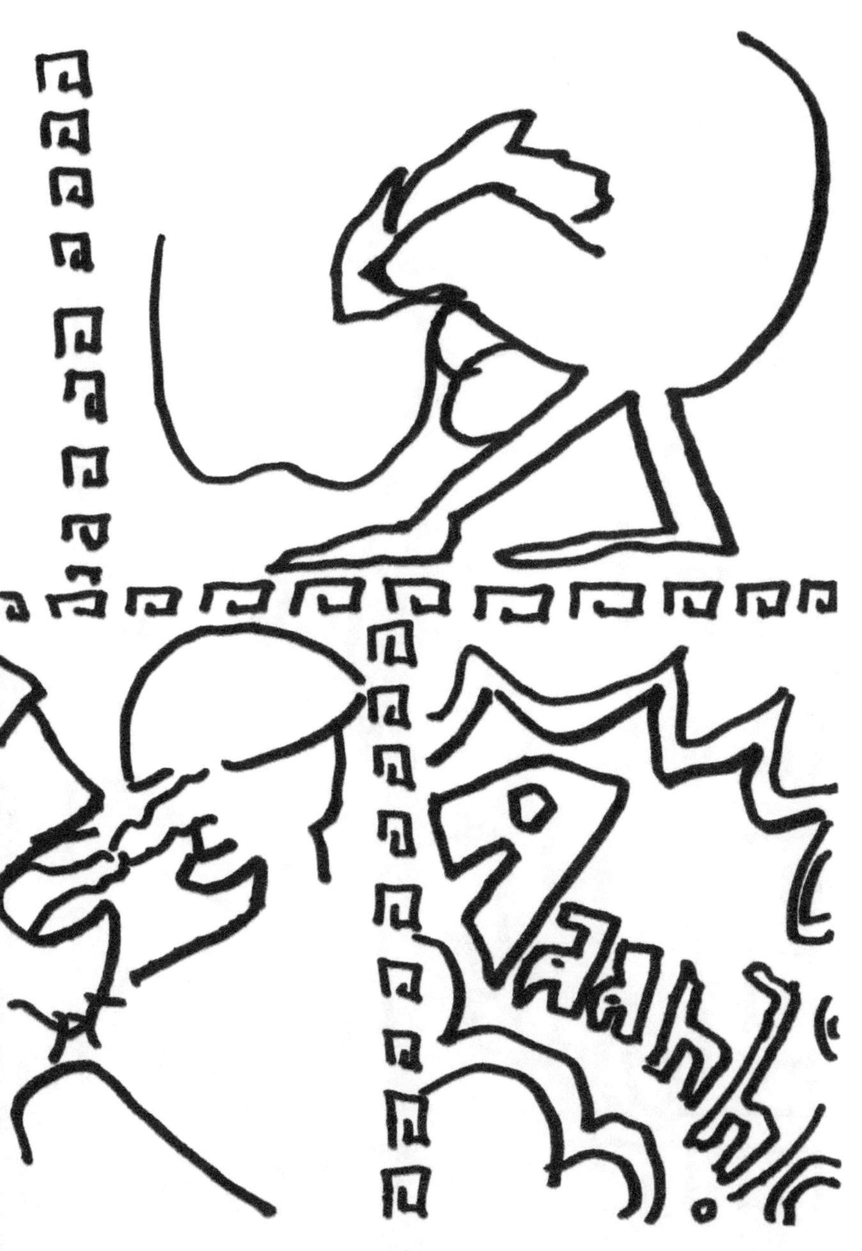

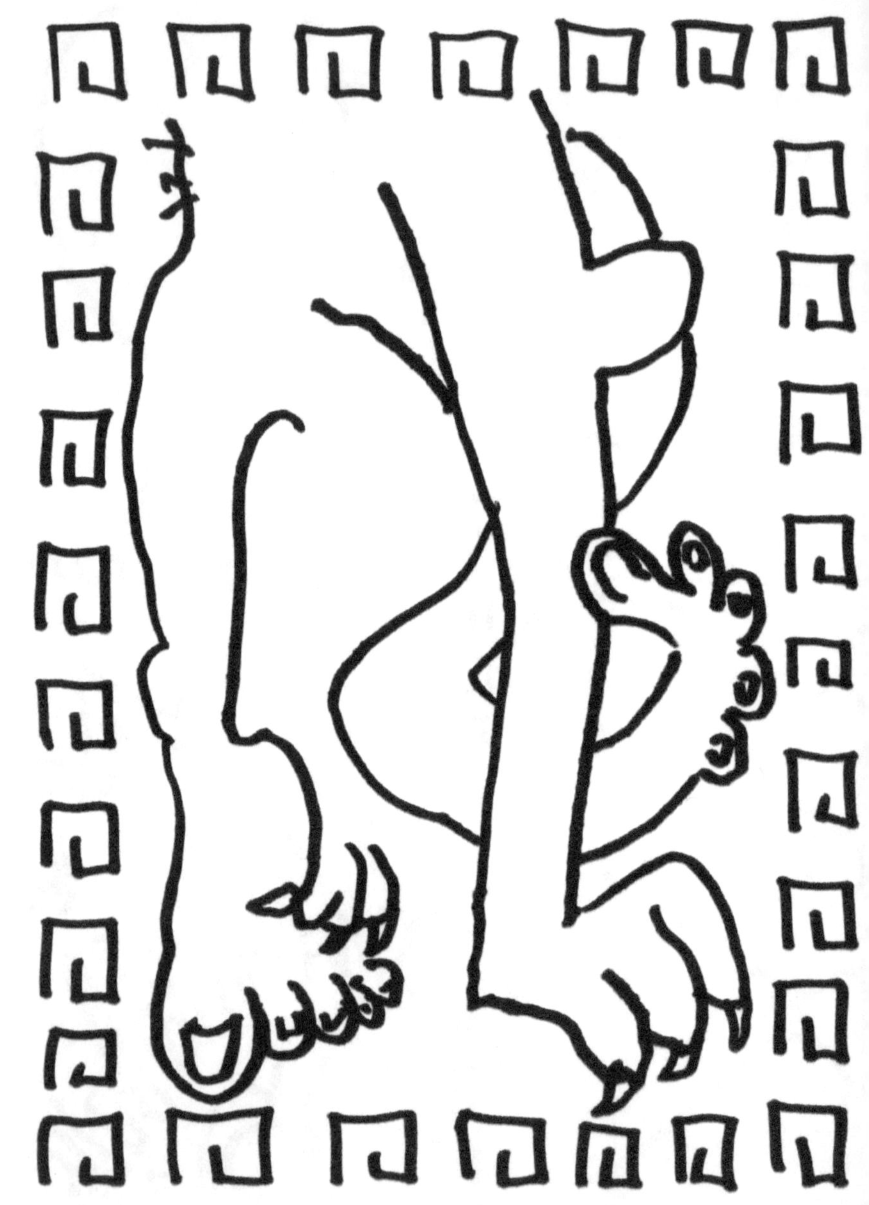

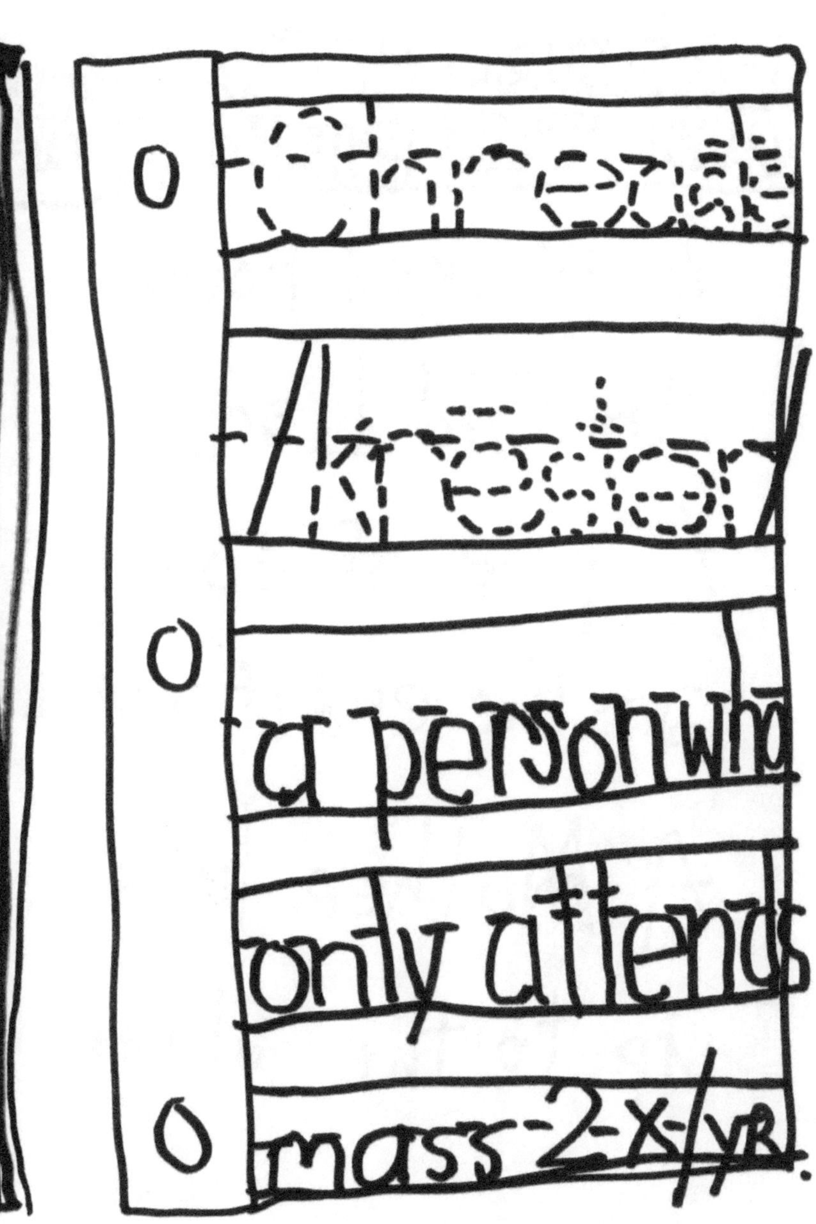

Christmas
X-factor
a person who
only attends
mass 2-X/yr.

PARABLE OF Two Women AND THE PILE OF COATS

A packed house.
An Old Lady.
A pile of coats
at the end of a bench.

A Mother looks
up to the alTer.

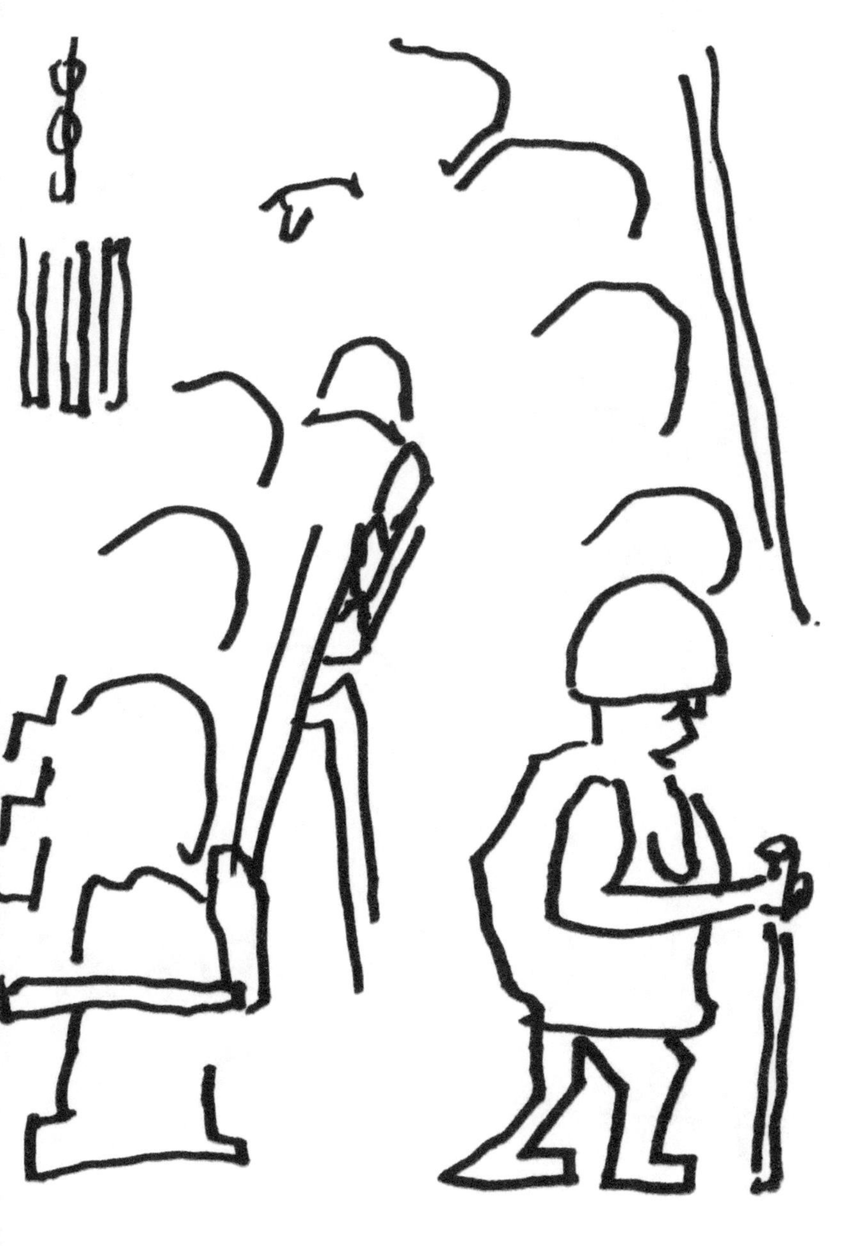

Old Lady (OL): (Looks Stops.

at coats)

Mother (M): (Looks

at old Lady)

OL: (looks at M)

M: (looks at coats)

OL: (looks at coats)

M:

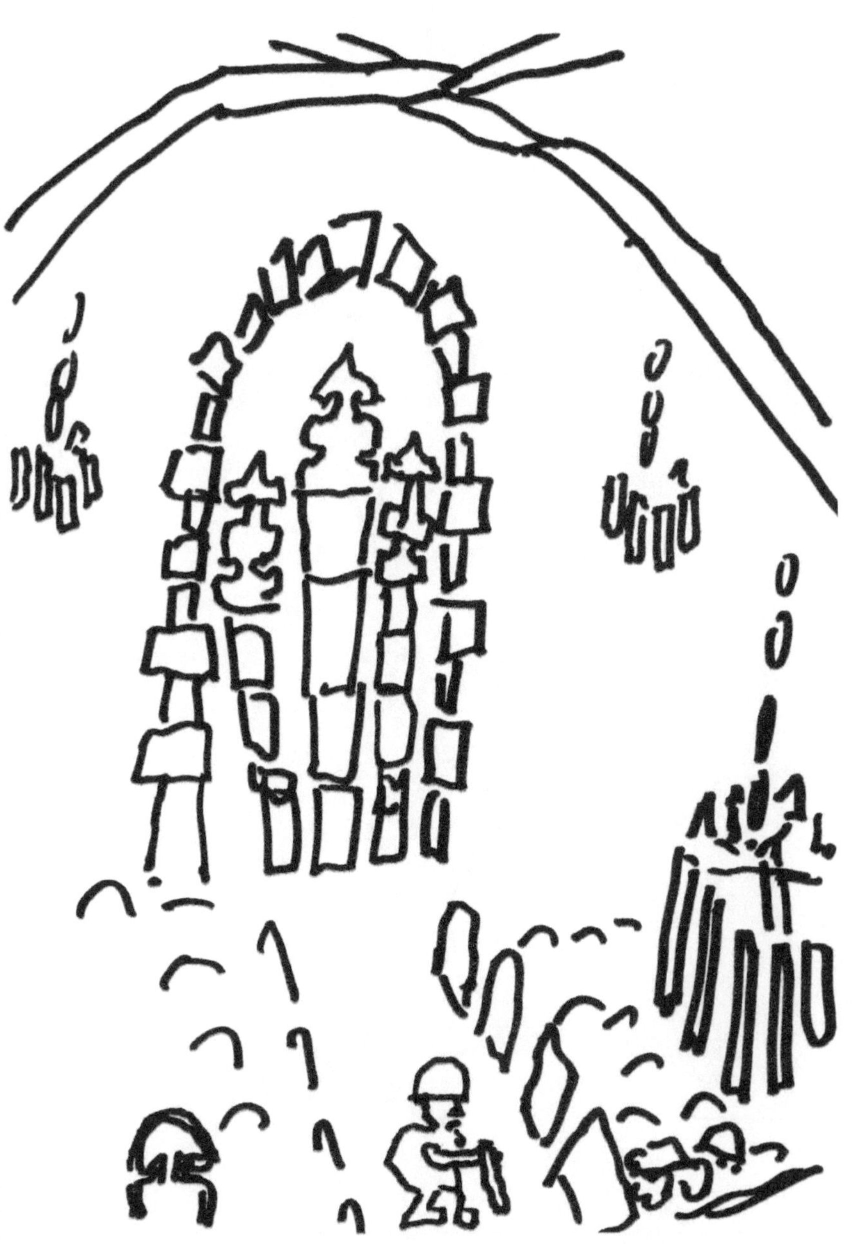

Looks
back

up
to
the
alter

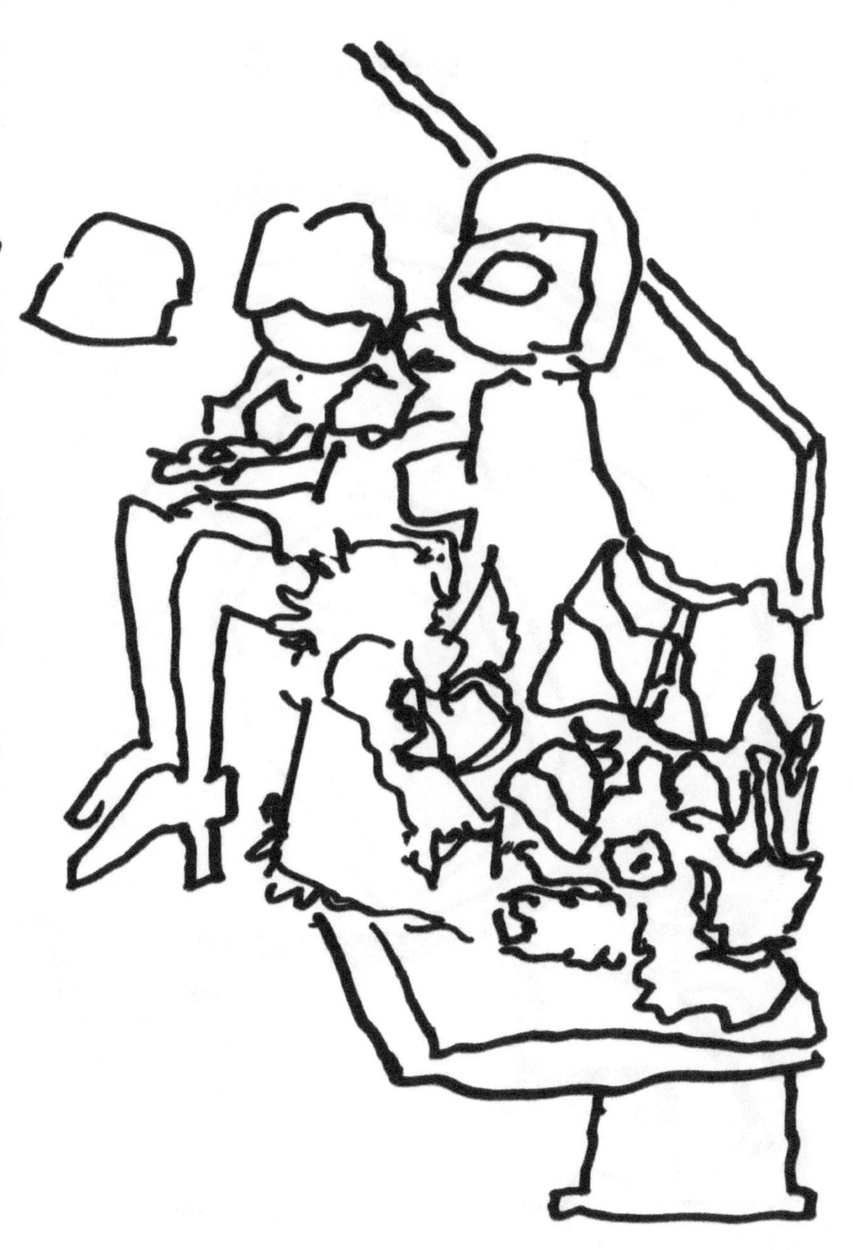

witness, in a ~~cothedral~~ full of
room witnesses,
7 yROld :
J.a.P

J.O.P : Do NOT
COVEt
that seat, child.
that angeR
will tuRn you
into the monsteR
that would tuRn
that motheR
into a fRog.

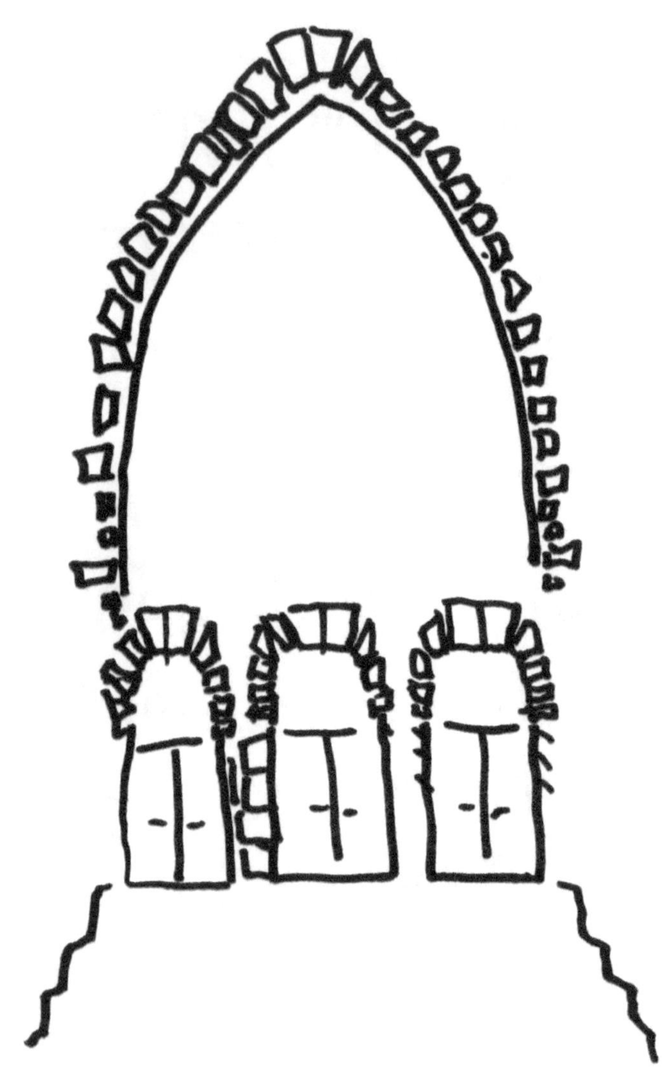

Also J.O.P:

Go and
thatch
the
shed
Roof.

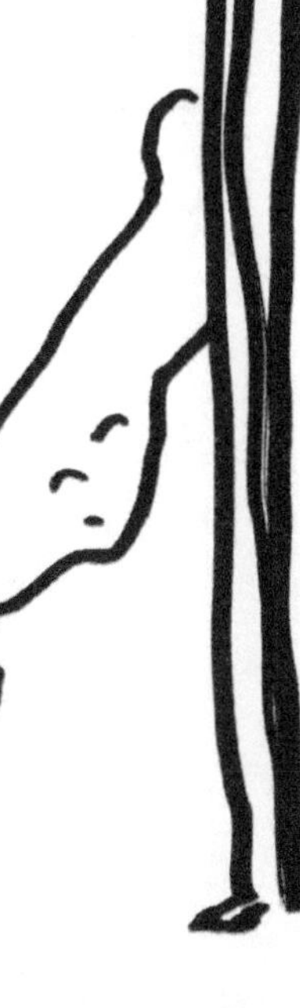

J.O.P: They're at the market.

Guest (G): they're at the market?

J.O.P: they're at the market.

Which, that, that, which
that which that witch with

WITCH!

G: Have
you
the
hemp
~~that~~ which that I have
Requested?

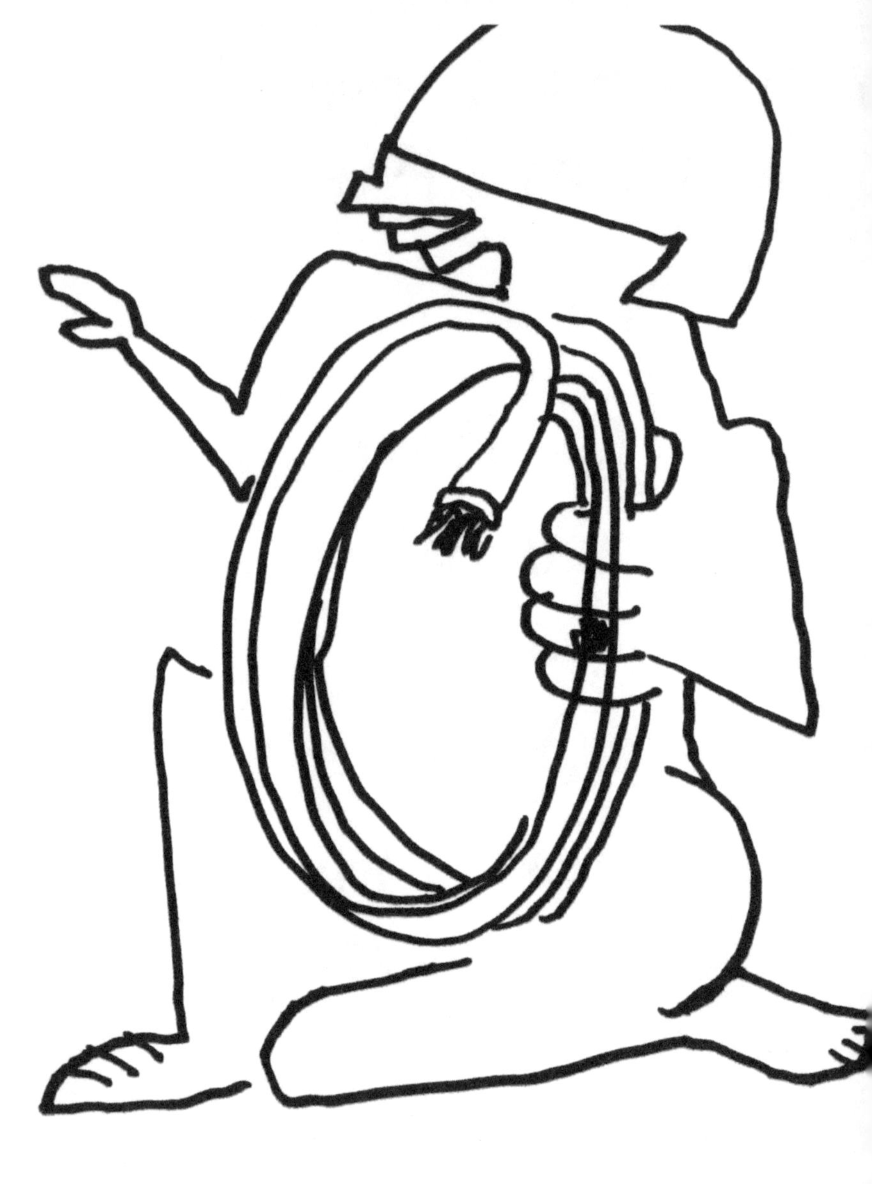

I DO.

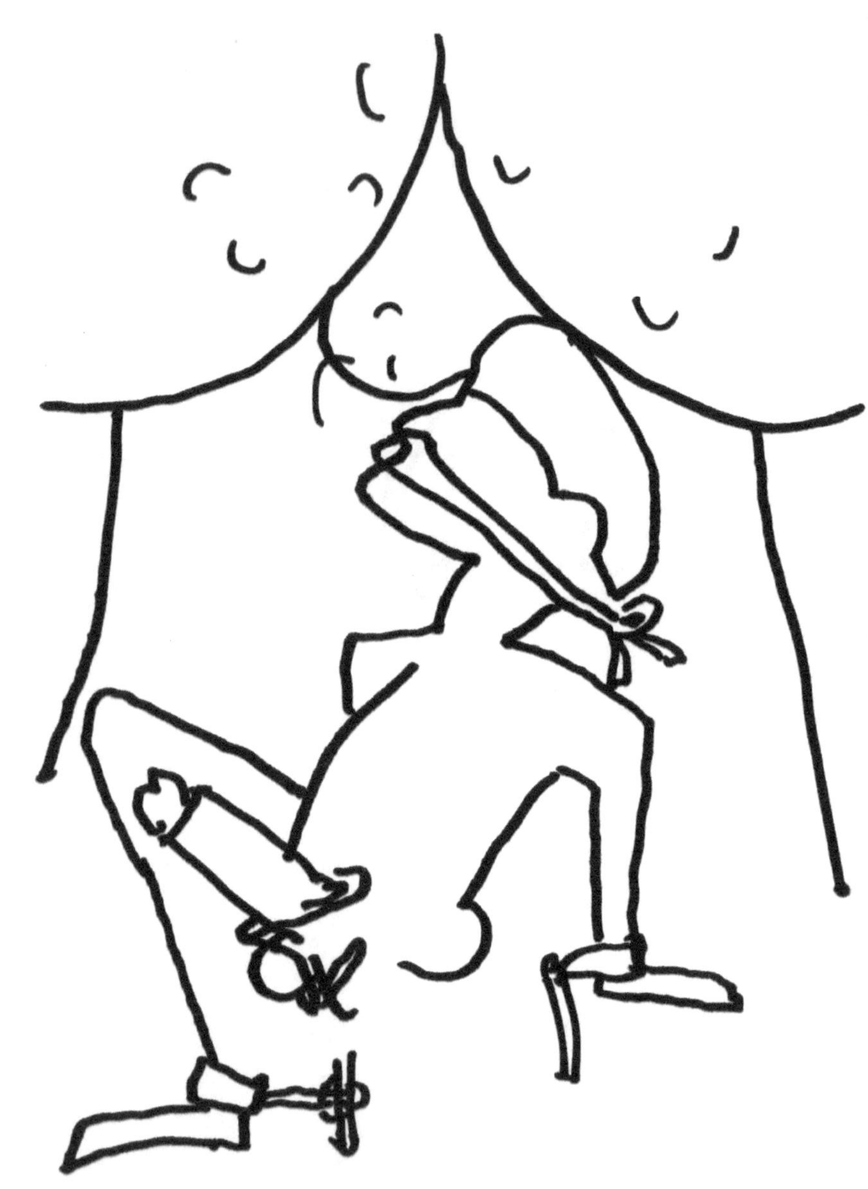

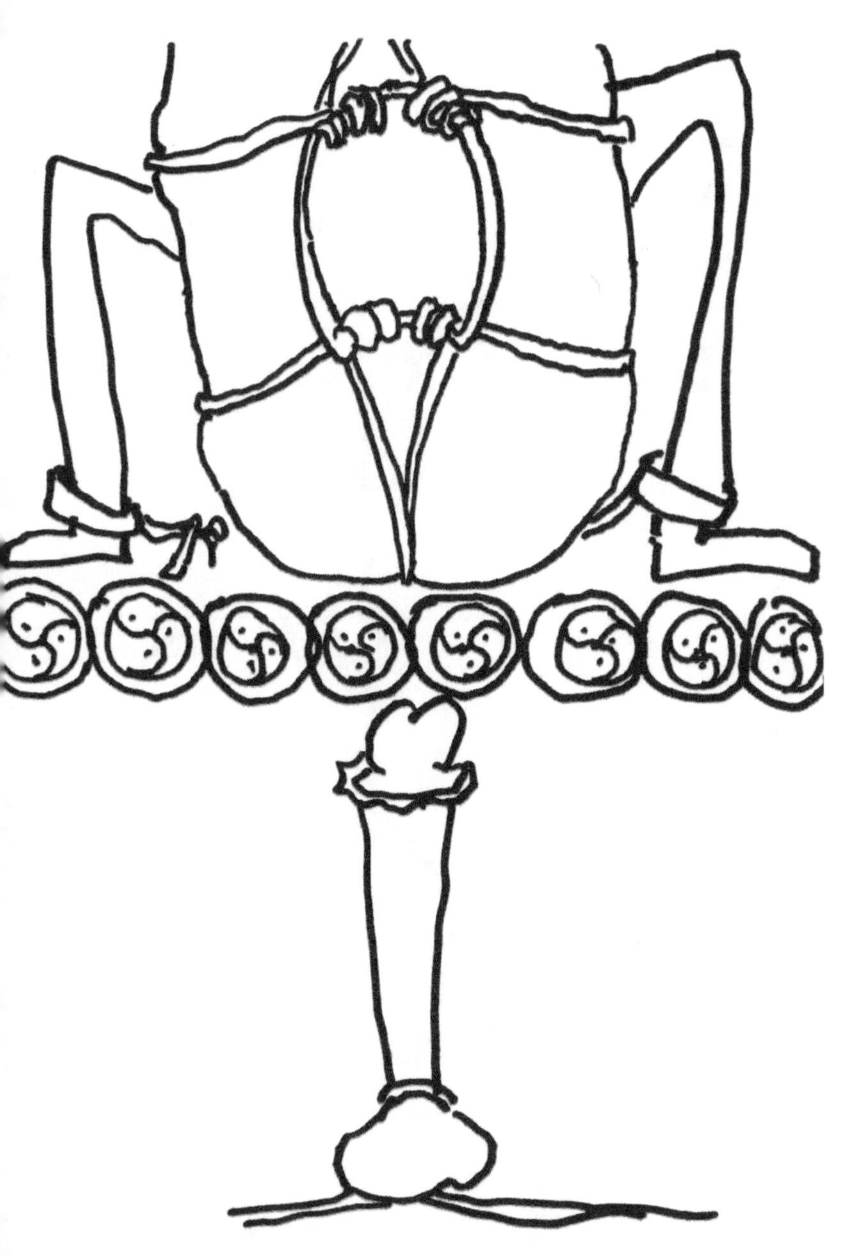

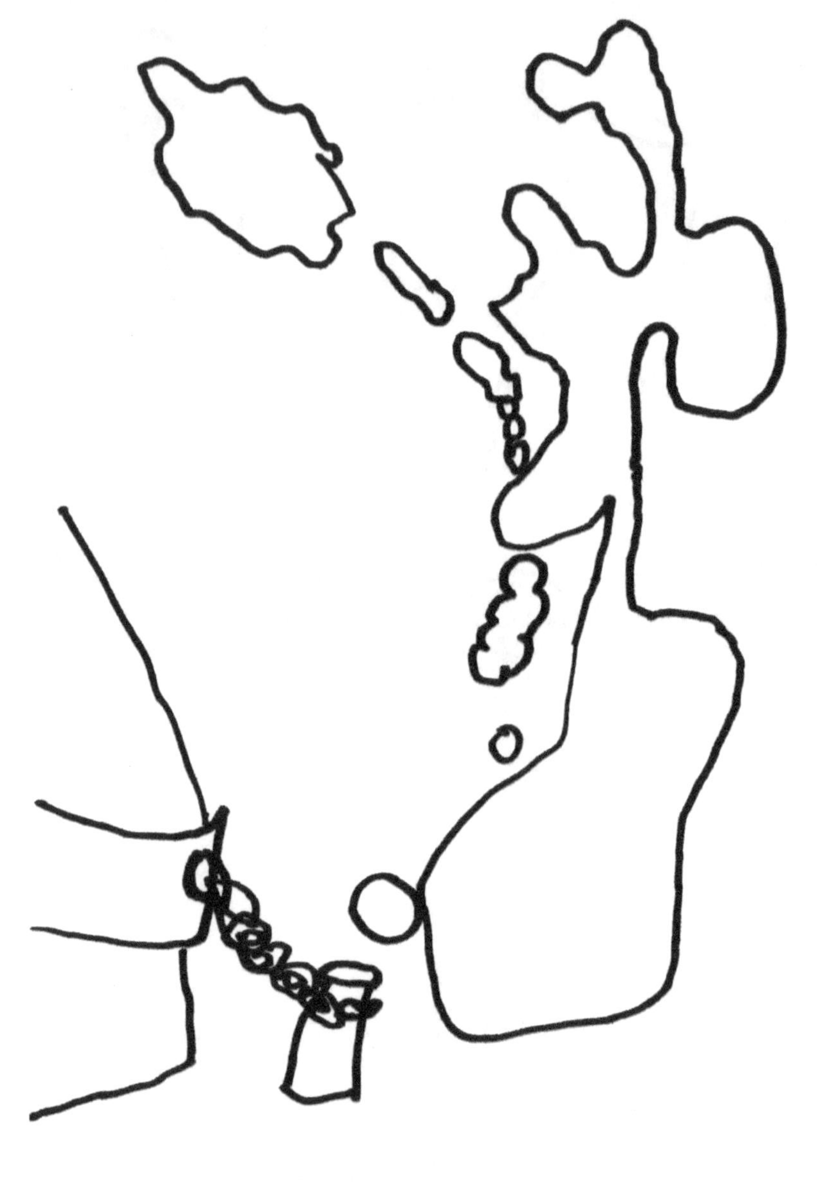

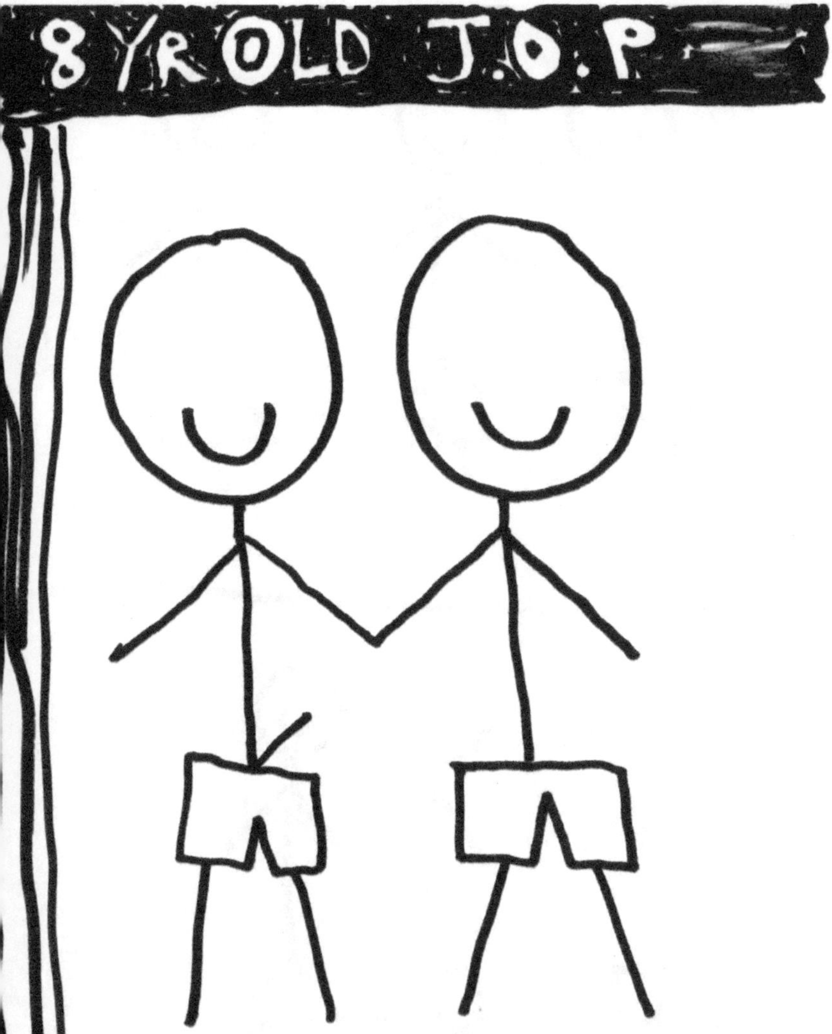

8 YR OLD J.O.P

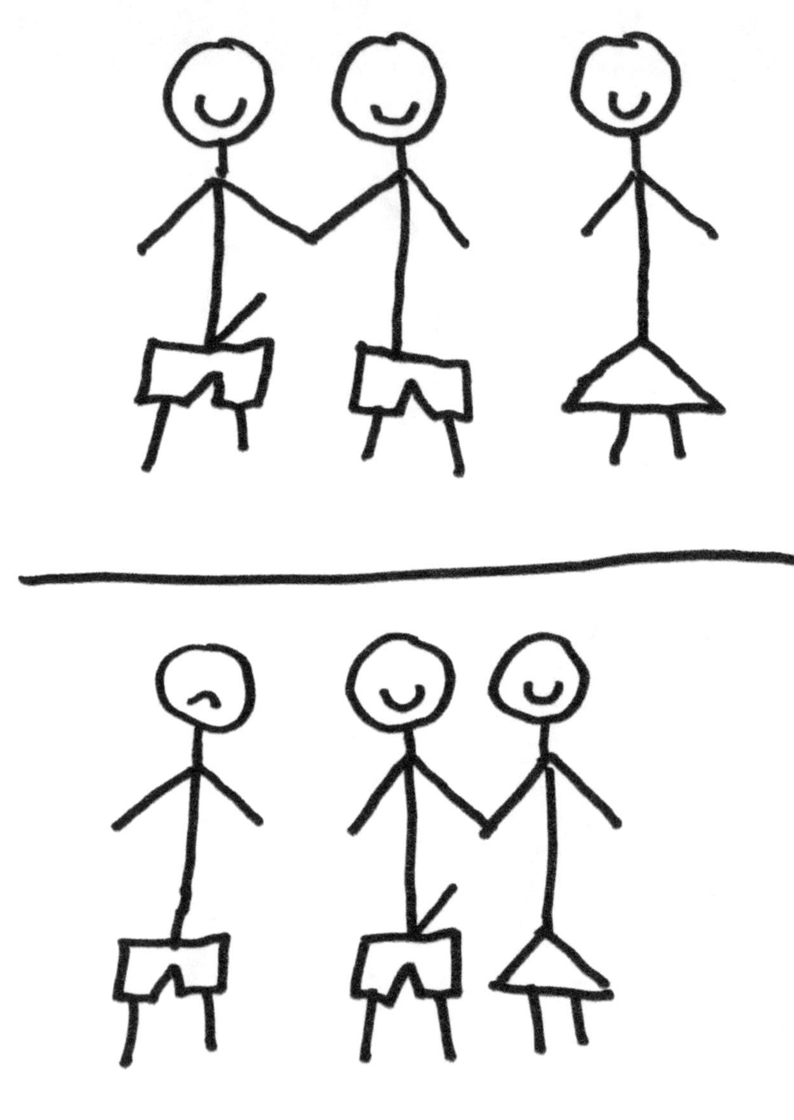

KING JAMES:

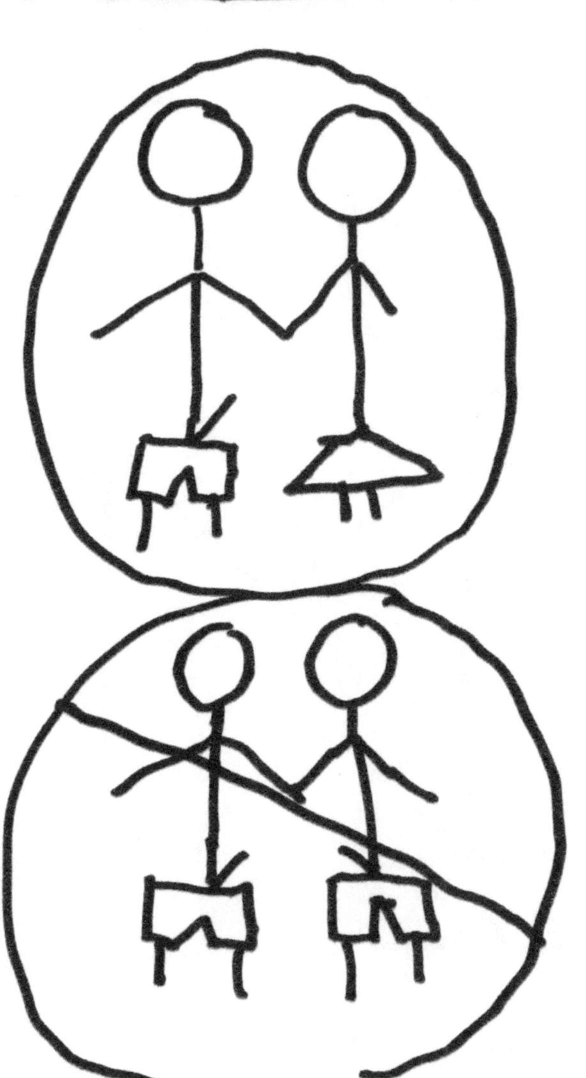

Also KING JAMES :

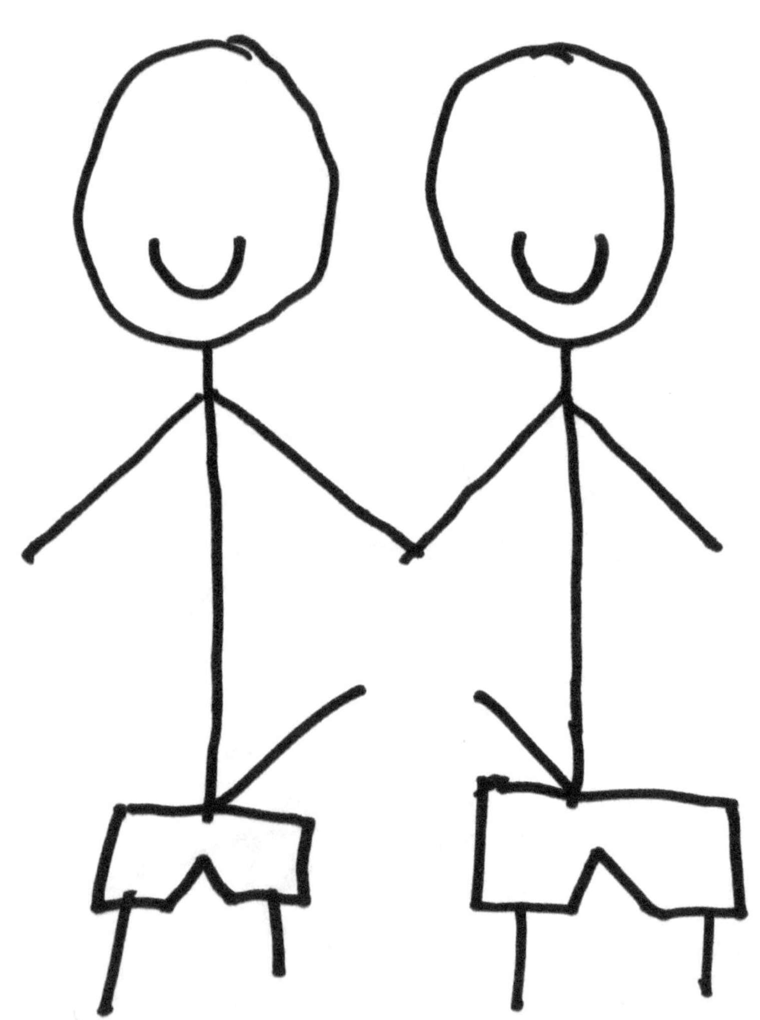

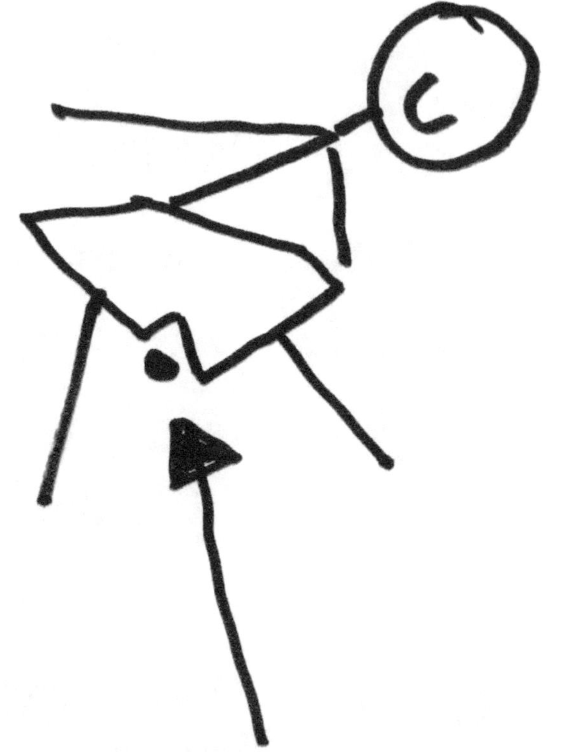

And furthermore, King James

The moral there,
kid, is never tell a
child that you love
them until third
grade ~~when~~ then tell
that same child that
you don't love him
anymore because
he has an innocent
crush on his best
friend, Brandon.

A BIG big
shout to
monotheism and
a special
mention for our
GREAT great
LEVITICUS

BROUGHT TO YOU IN PART B
DEFENSE
MECHANISMS
Flash Cards

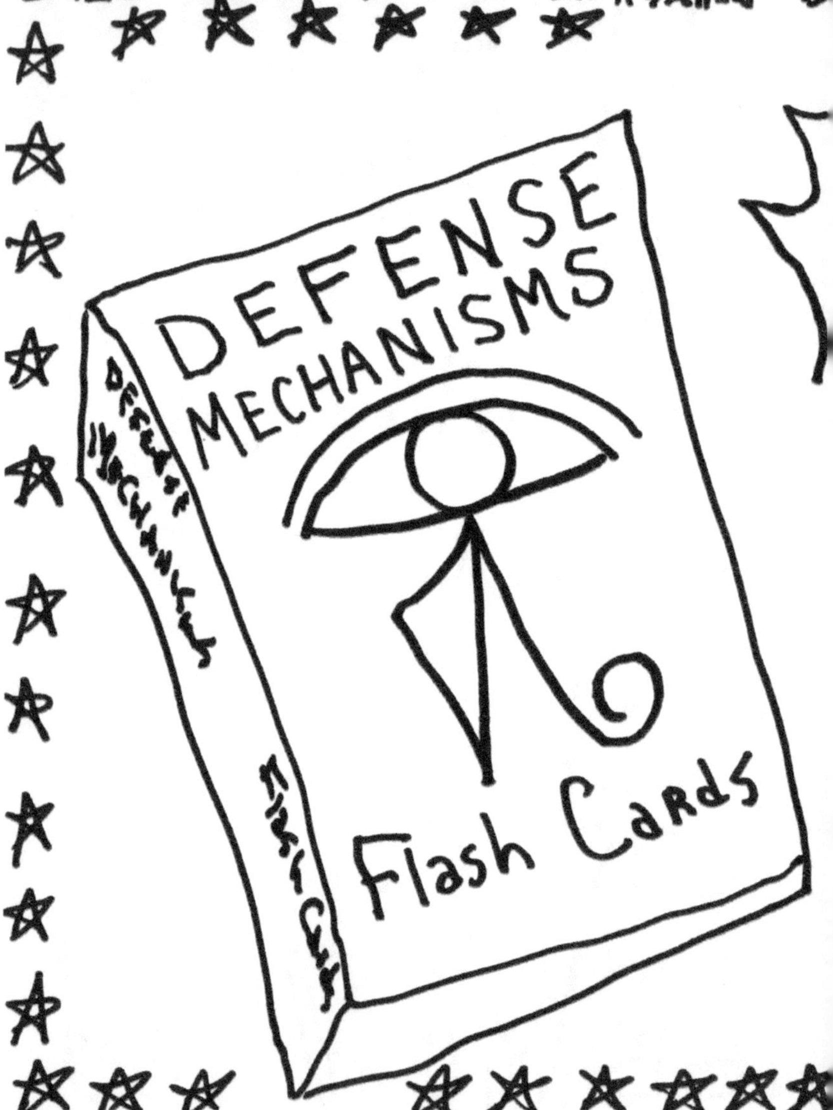

$... and by Viewers Like You!
With Popular Favorites
Repression
Regression
Reaction Formation
• Denial
• Projection
• Displacement
• Rationalization

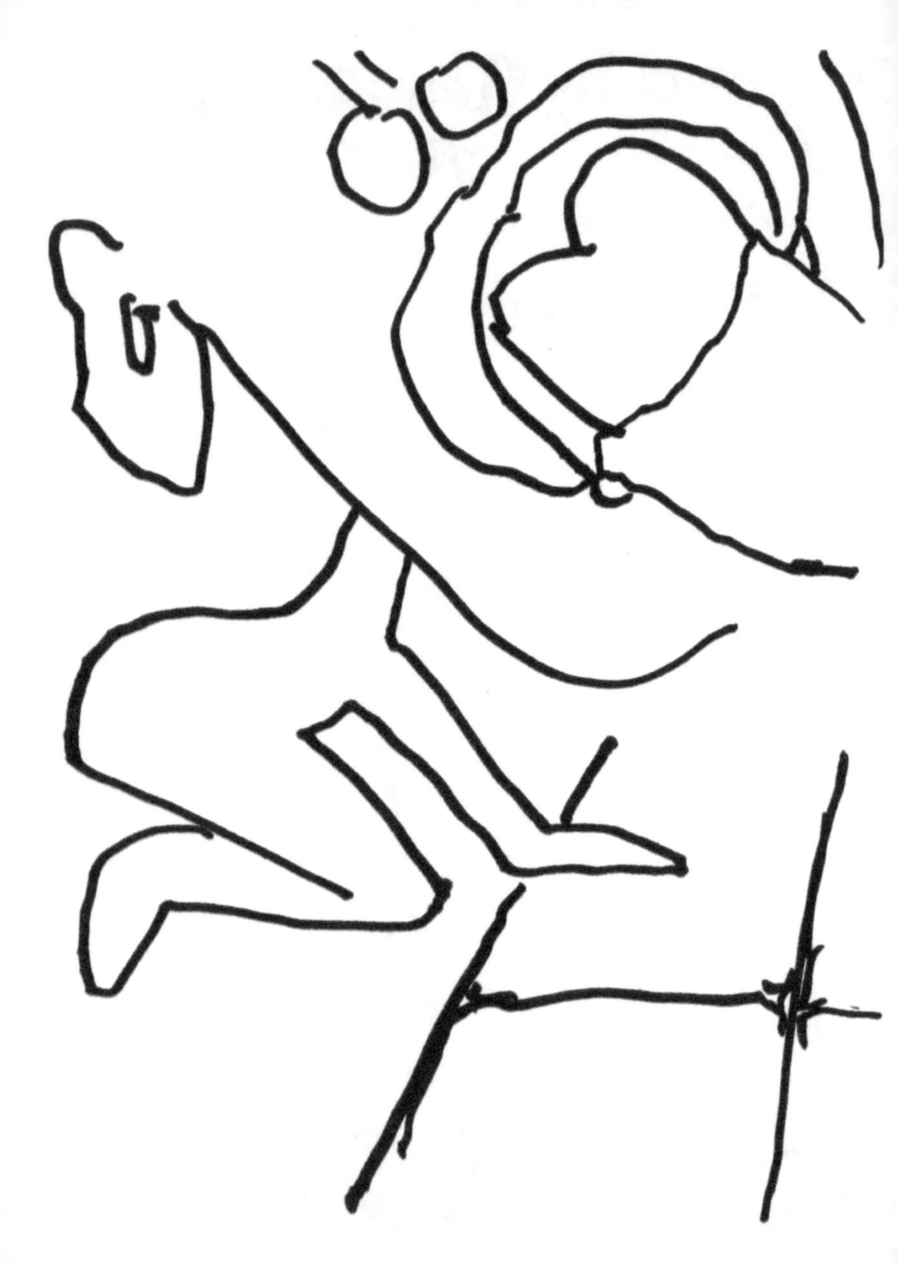

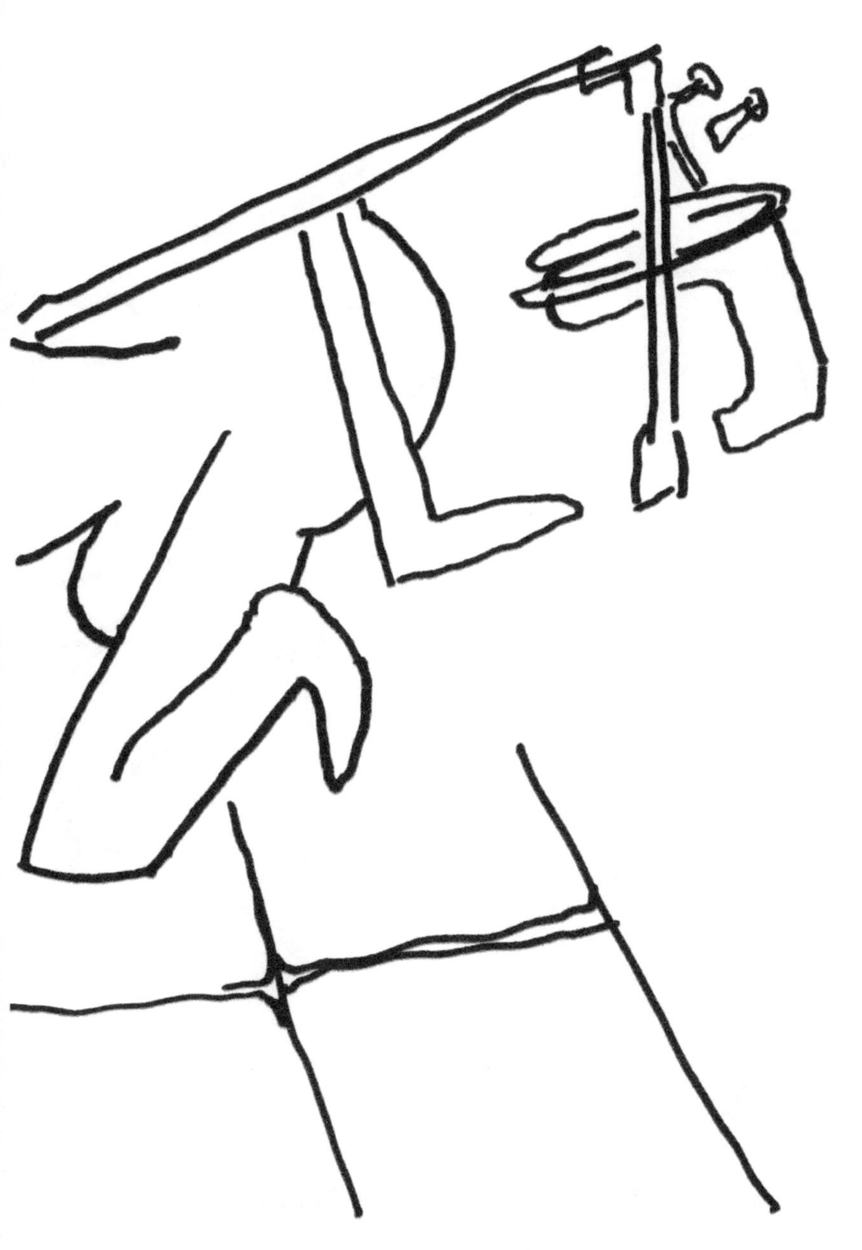

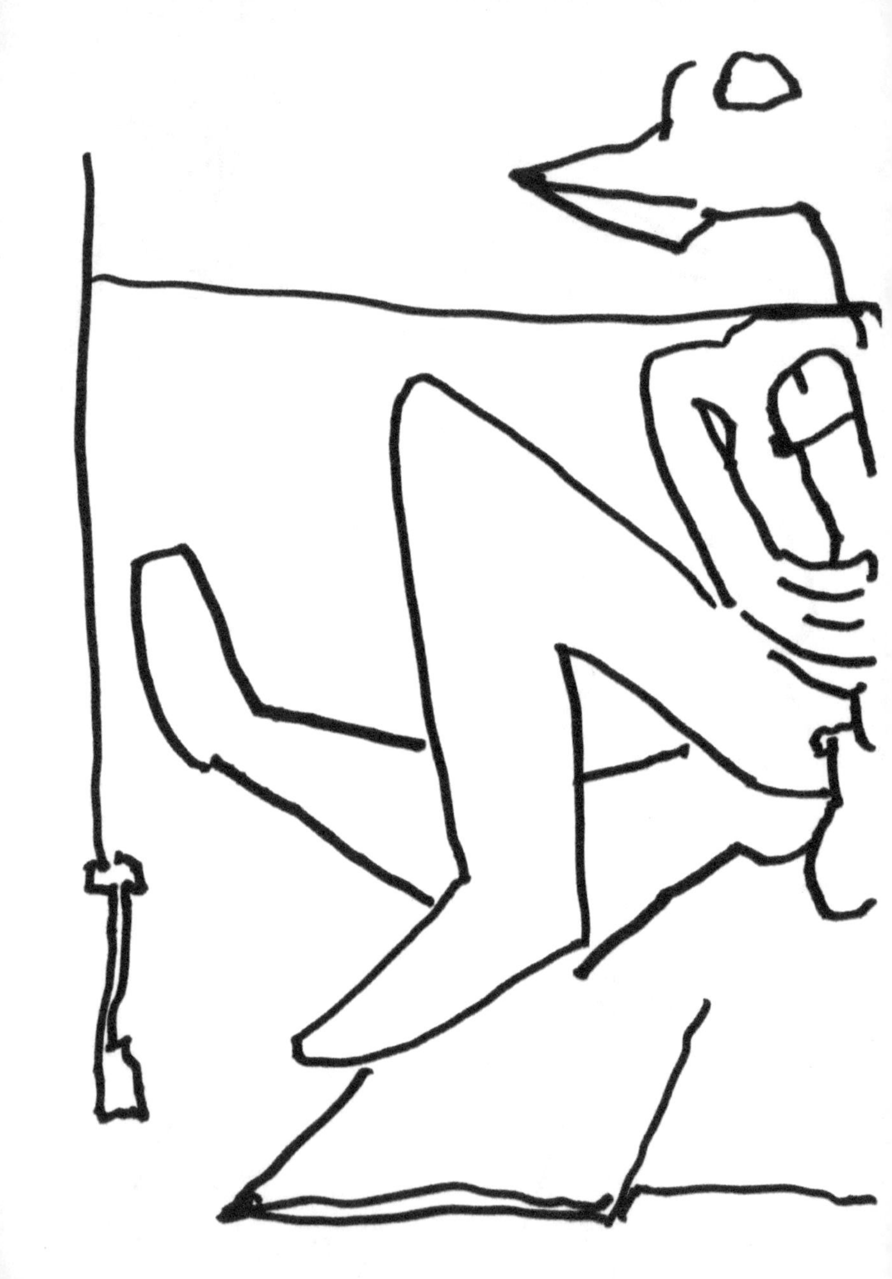

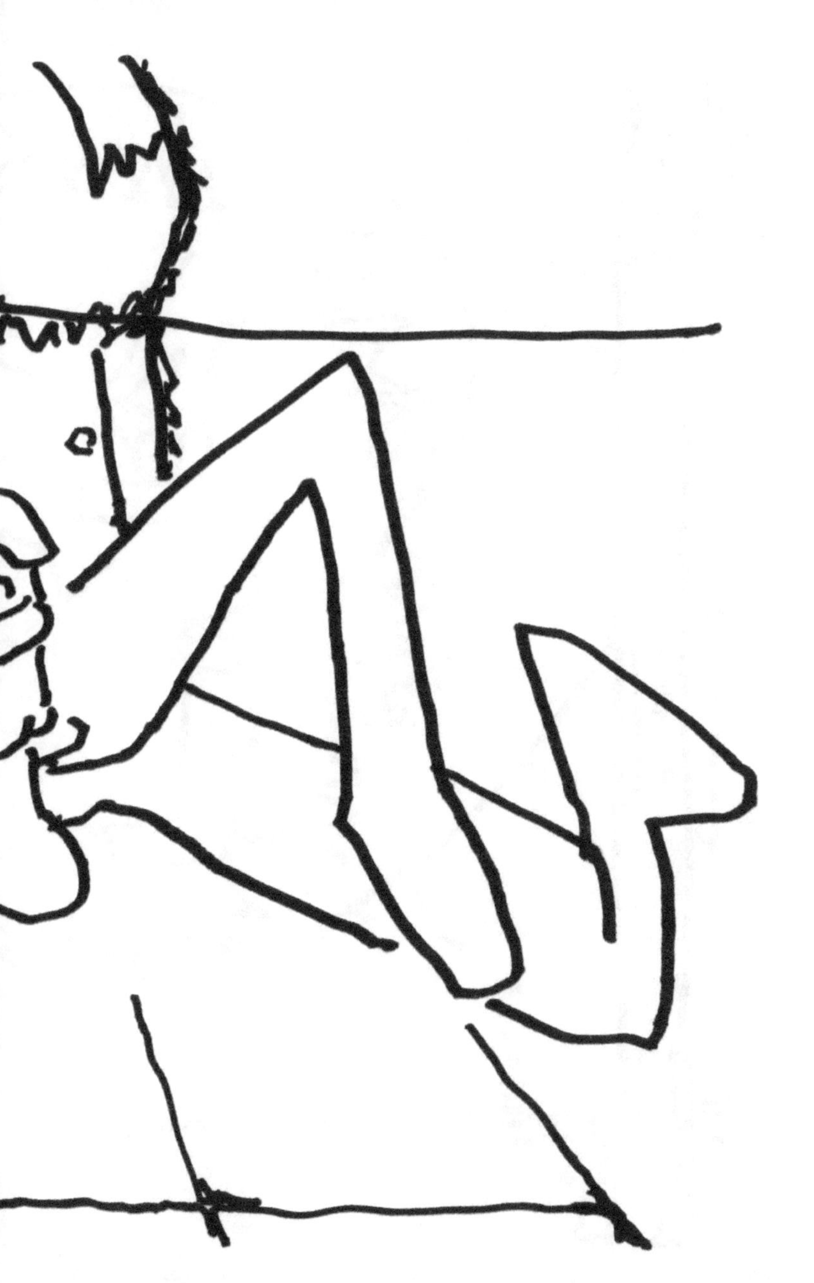

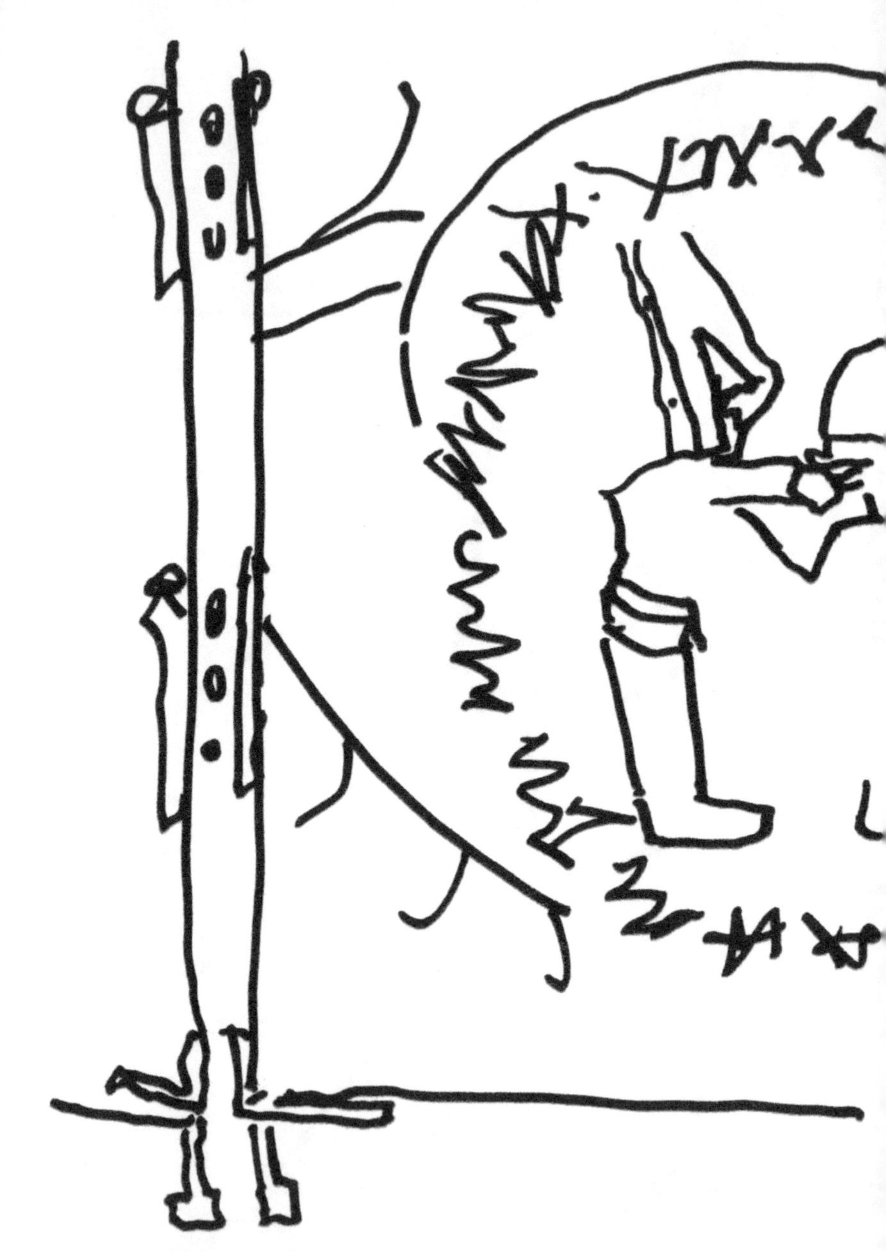

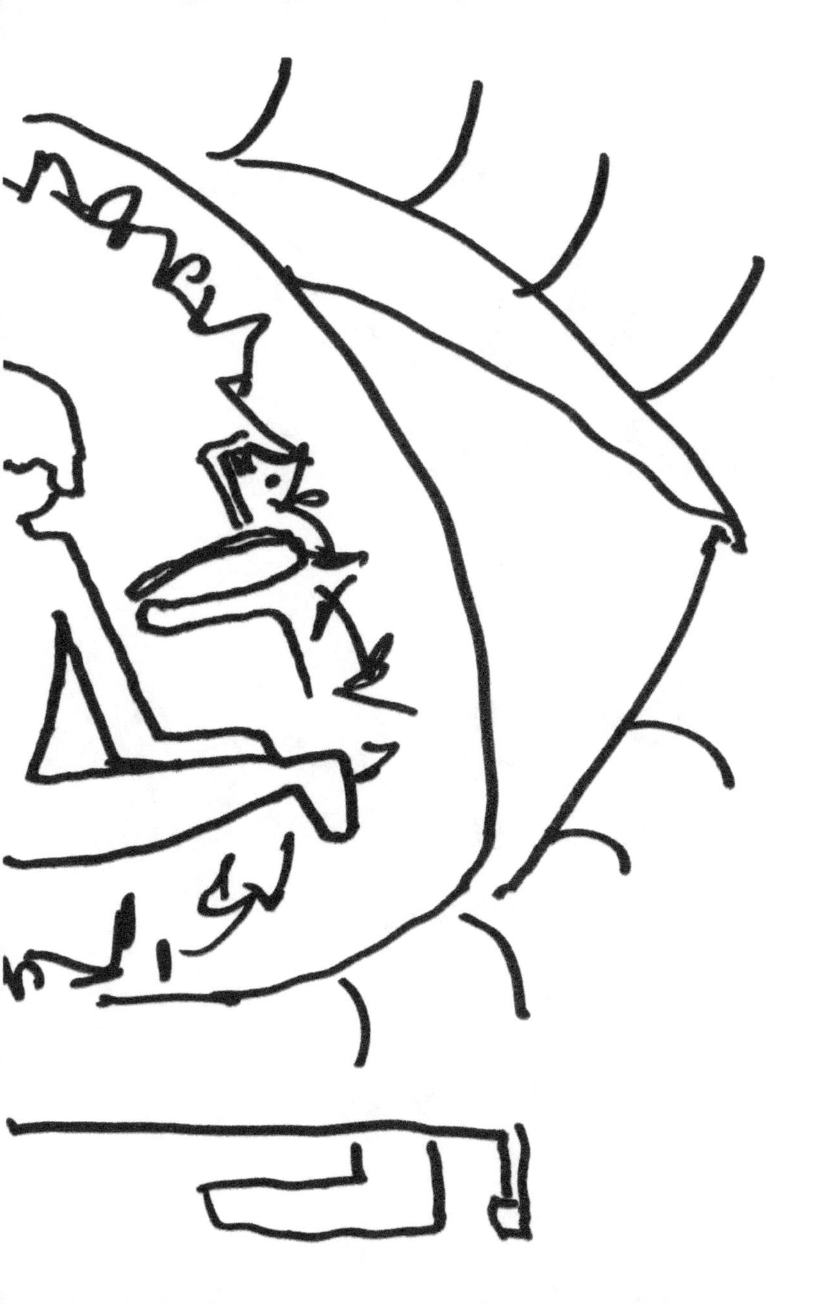

AIDE: Senator, what about this gay shit bill?

Senator: Big Nay

Also Senator, about to finish.
AIDE: You want it in your mouth, Sir?

Senator: Yay Yay Yay

Buy it.
Sell it.
Punish it.
Confuse,
Control it.

PARABLE OF THEGREA

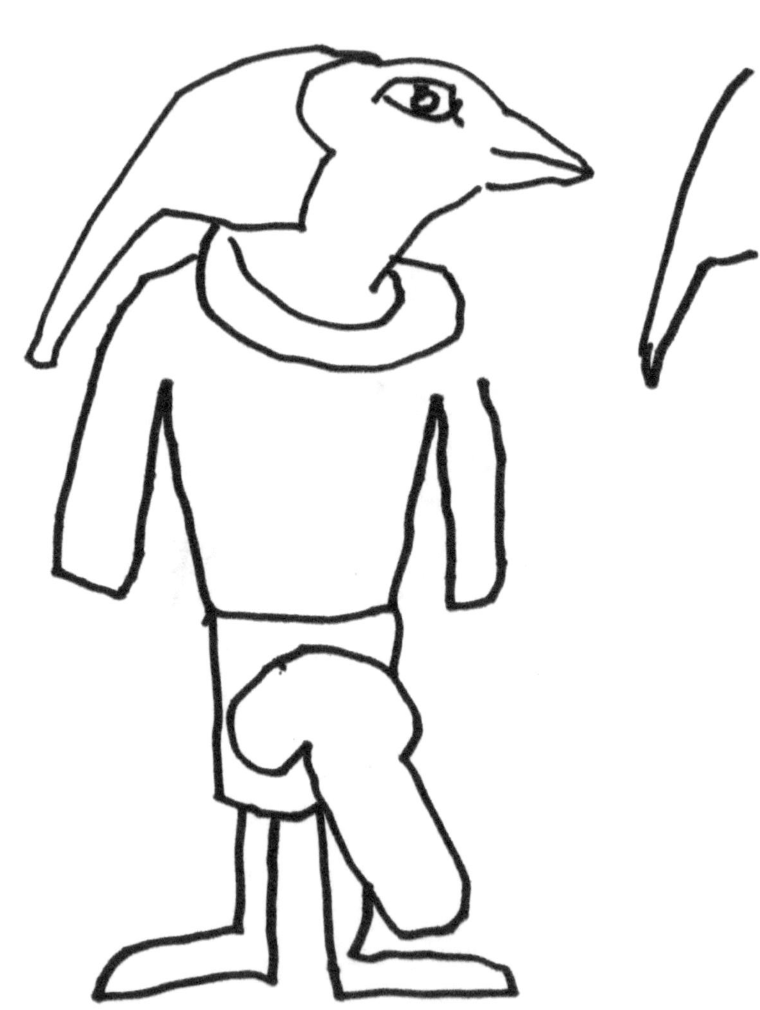

T M~~[scribbled out]~~ BAIT n Switch ISSIONARY

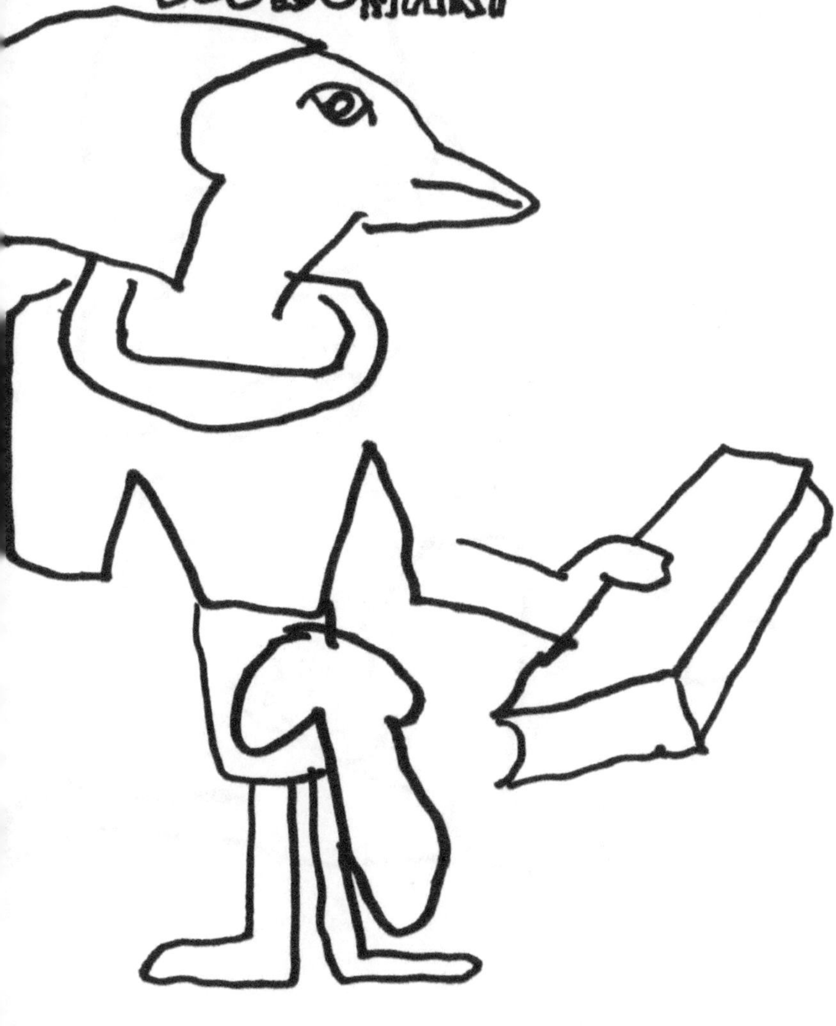

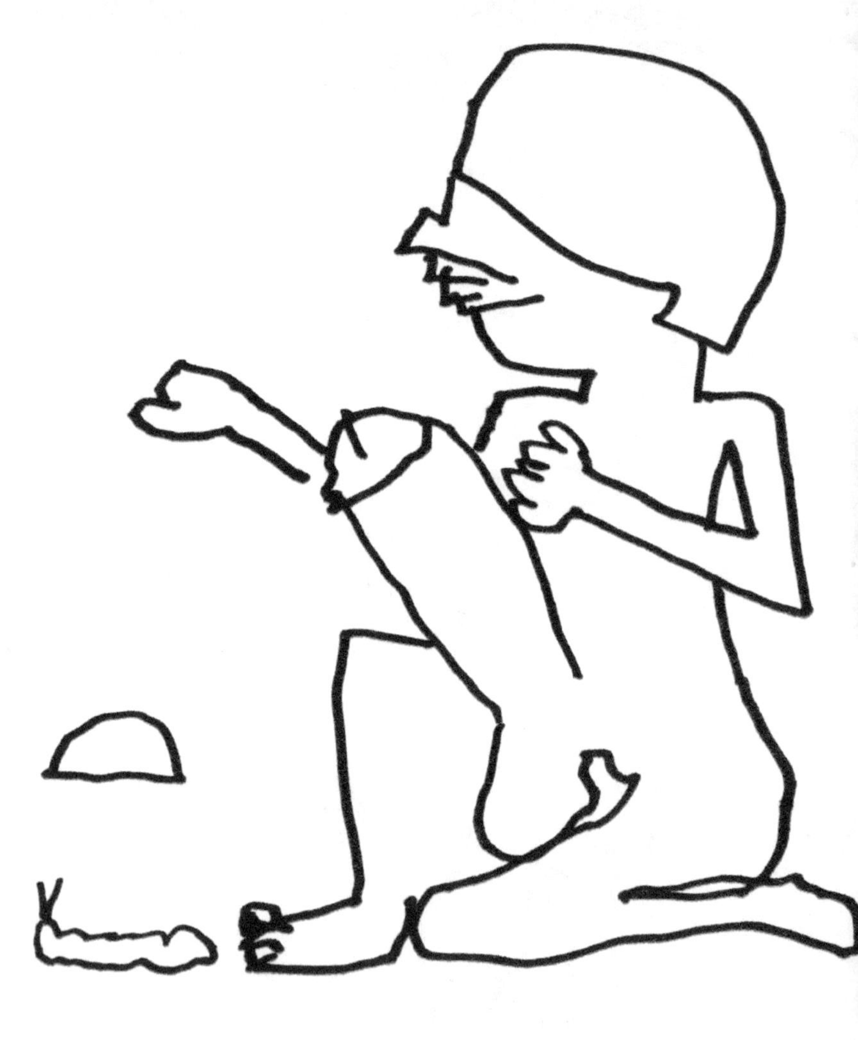

9 (OR 10) YR OLD: Two
J.O.P
very handsome ~~men~~
men came to
Uncle's door.
They had in
their hand
a book.
Uncle seemed very
pleased to meet them.

9 (OR 10) YR OLD : He'd
  J.O.P (cont.)
have listenend to them
speak for hours, just
watching their mouths
move. The tendons in
their necks, the rise
and fell of each breath
the growing anticipation,
  their exhuberance,
    the heat from -...
our shadows grew and
Uncle asked could they
come another time.
We had today, unfortunately
  a prior appointment.

the

two

~~boys~~ youngmen

said

" yes, "

they'd come

again the

following week.

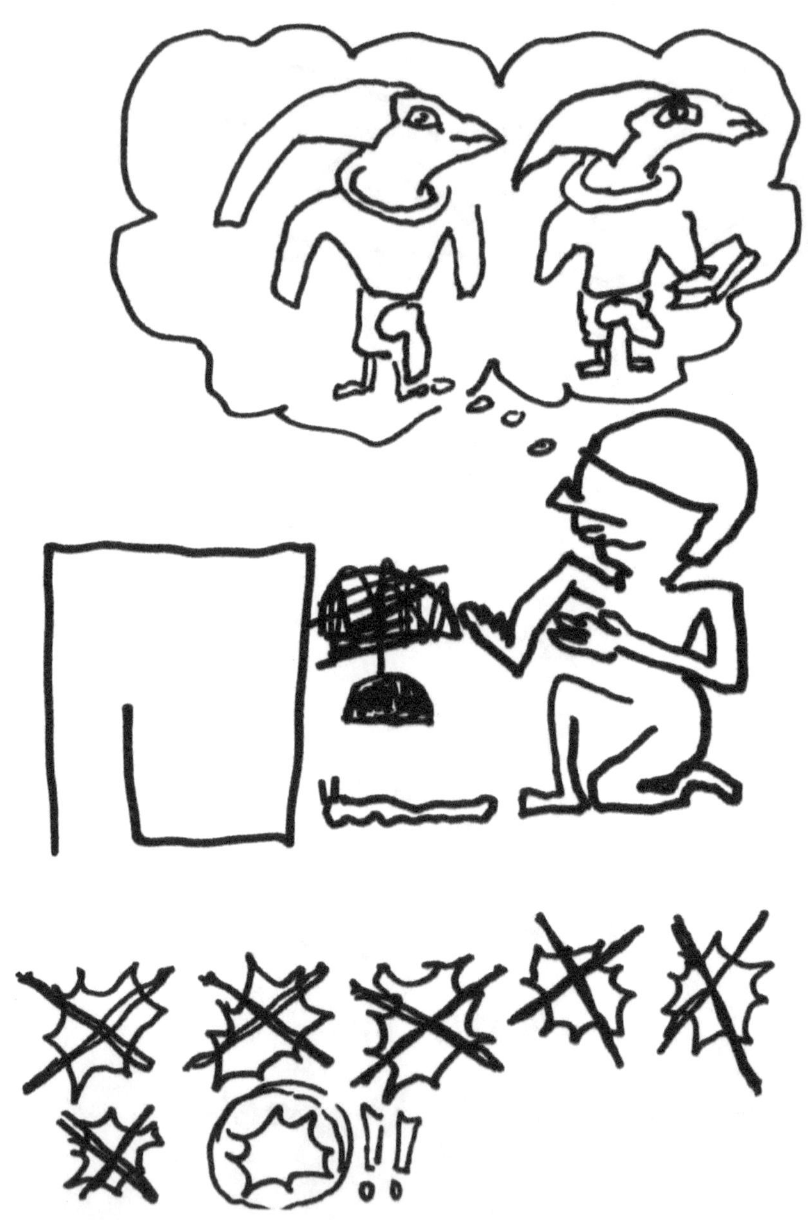

9 (OR 10) YR OLD:
J.O. P(cont.)

Finally, the day
of their return
arrived. Uncle
waited by the
front door.
Eventually, after
many hours, two
men appeared.
They, too, had in
their hand a
book, the same
book that the
two very hot
men had
carried.

"J.O.P?" They asked.

"Yes," Uncle Replied.

"You Requested us?"

"Not you."

~~"Where Are the other dudes?"~~

"I Requested the other dudes."

"What about the book?"

~~"Away with you."~~

~~"..."~~

"No. Thank you. You may go now."

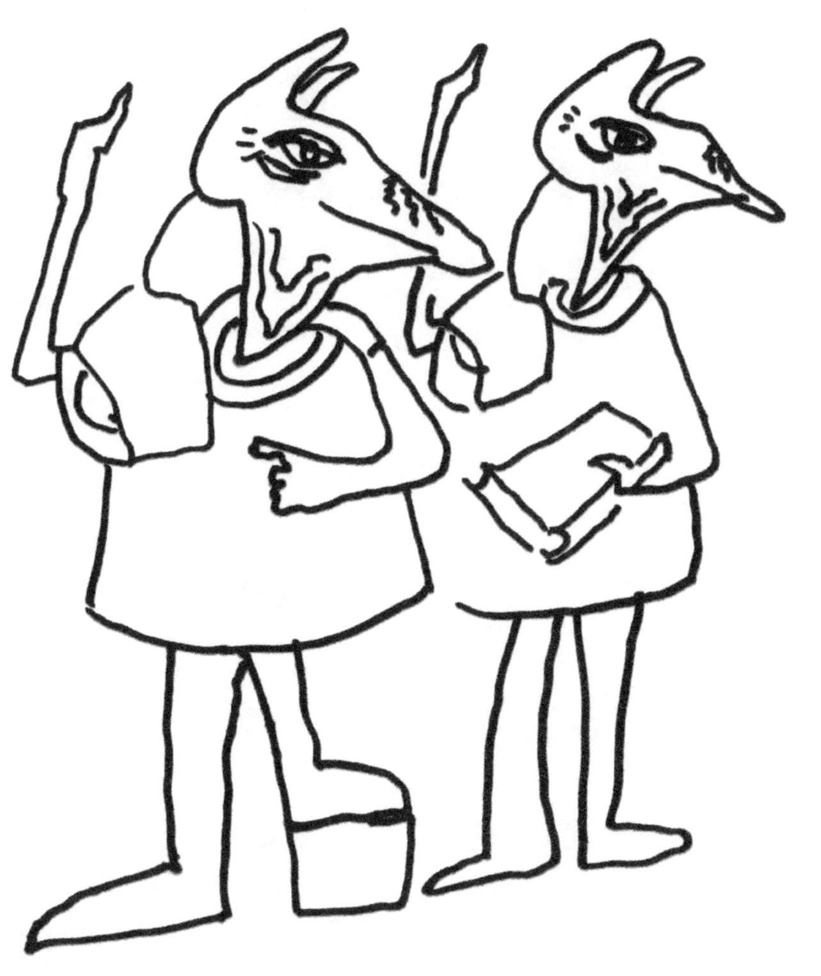

9 (OR 10) YR OLD: Uncle,
    J.O.P
            would it
not have been
easier to claim
   they to be mistaken
   in your identity?

J.O.P: Little one,

We shalt not
bear false
witness.

Also J.O.P:

The
stable
gutters
Remain
~~unm~~clogged.

Do, Remedy
that.

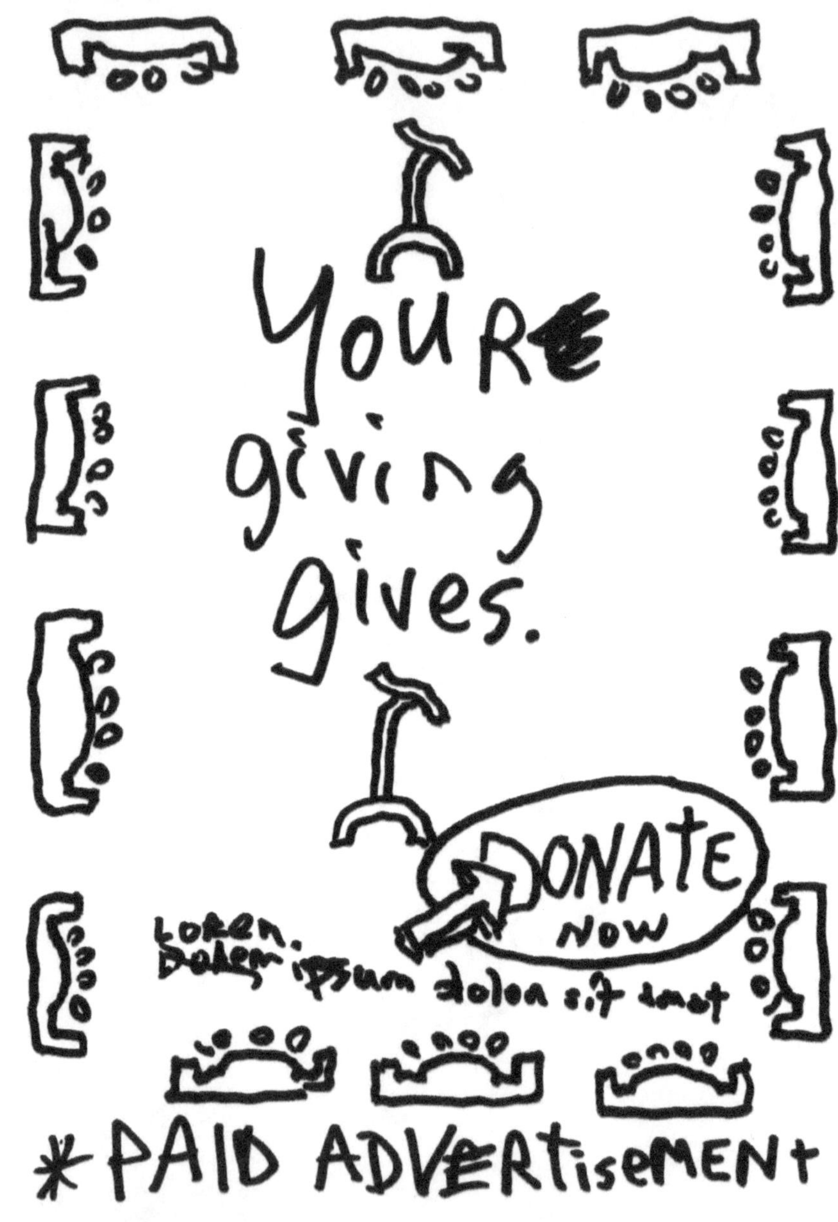
You're
giving
gives.
DONATE
NOW
Lorem.
Dolor ipsum dolor sit amet
* PAID ADVERTISEMENT

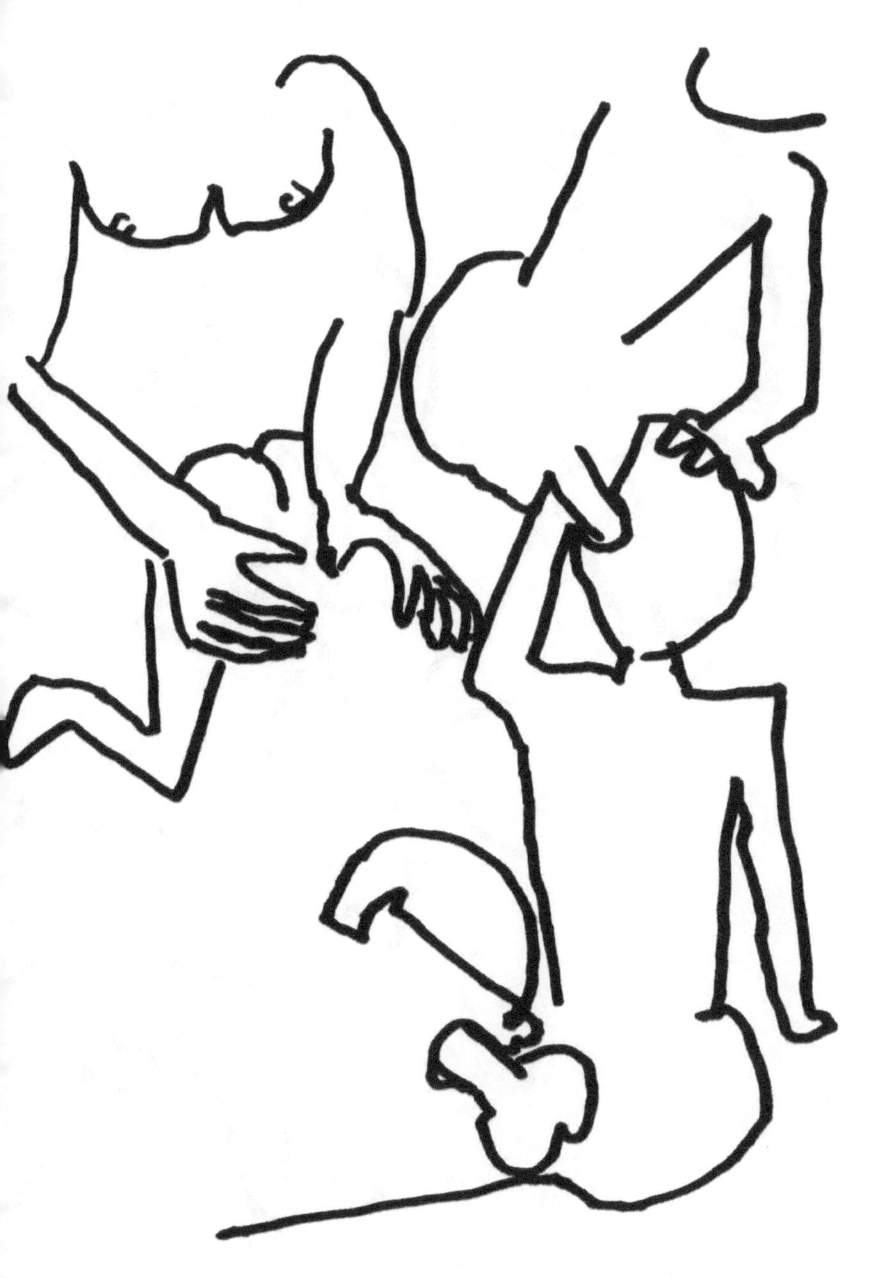

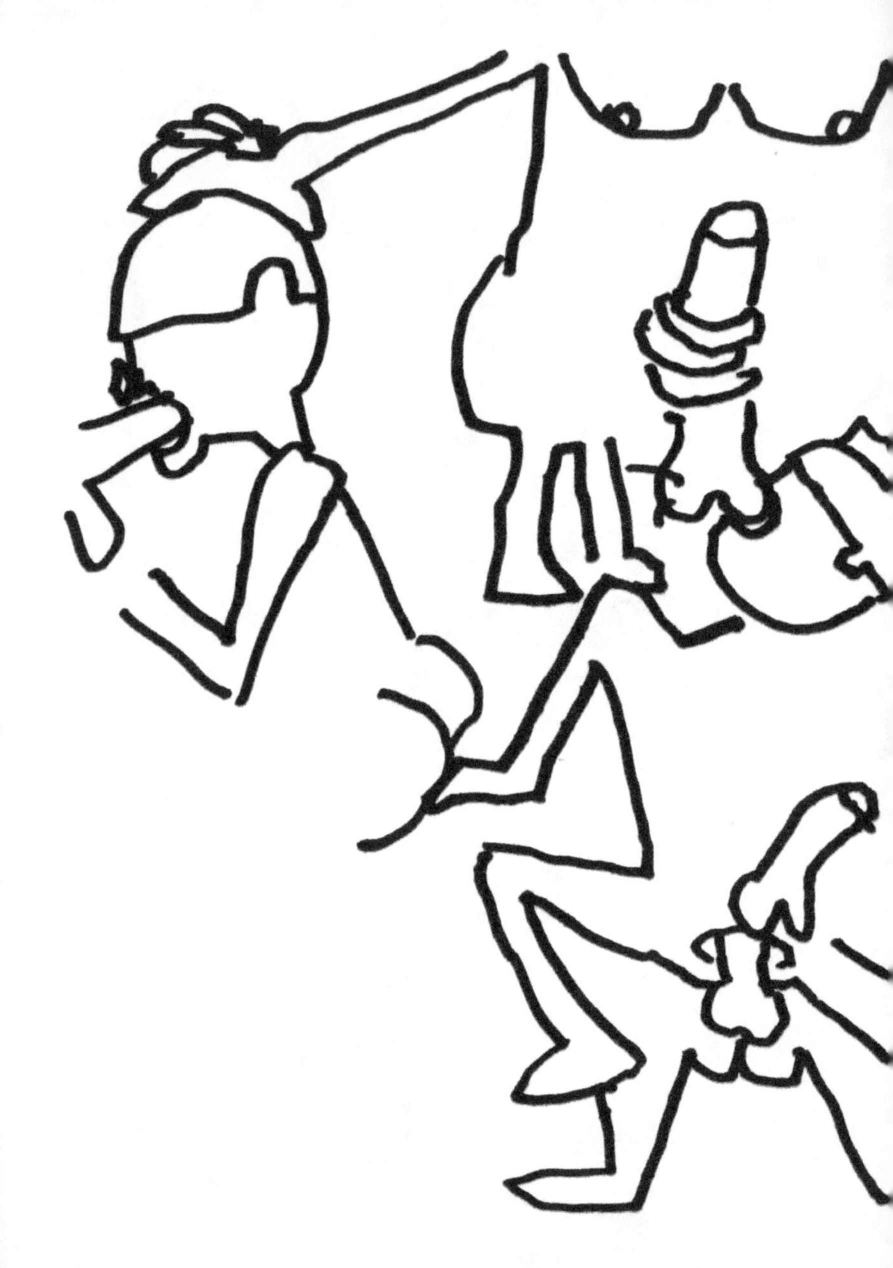

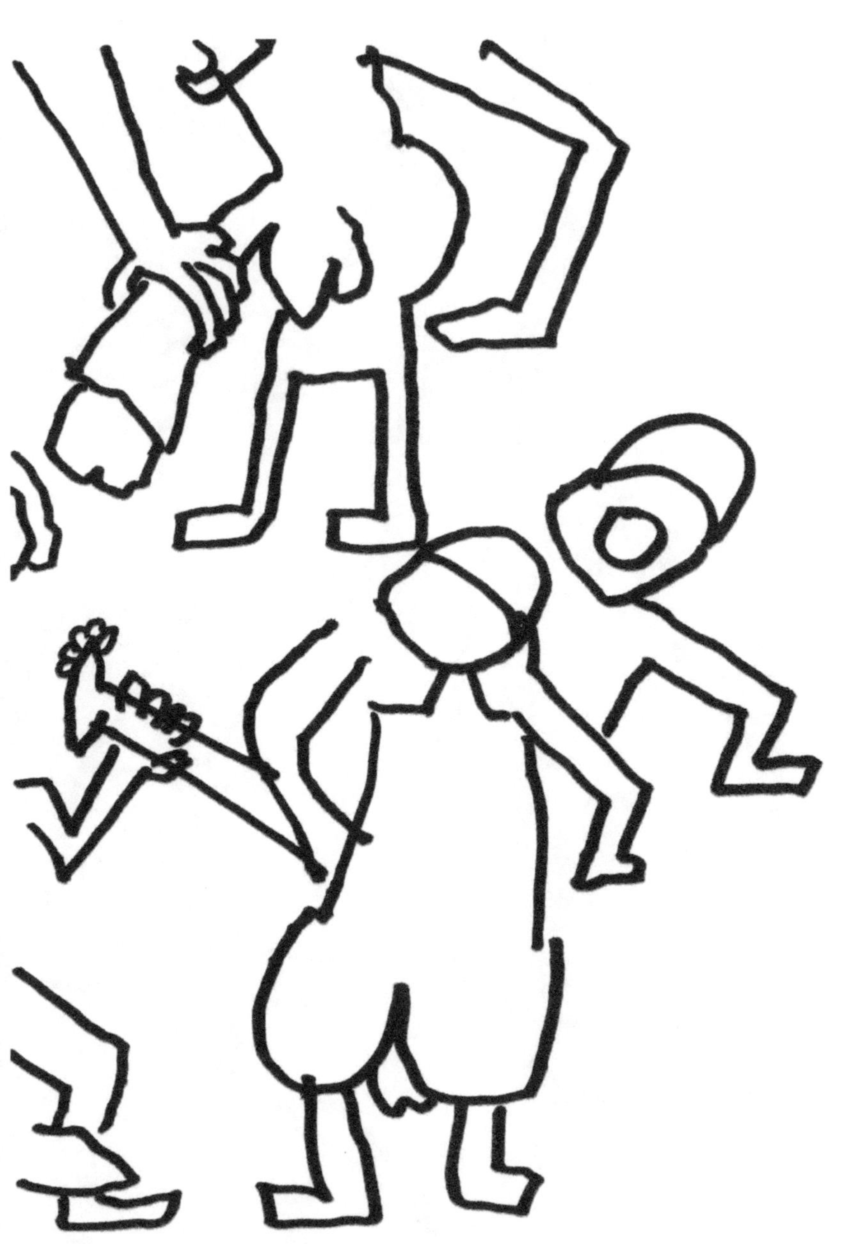

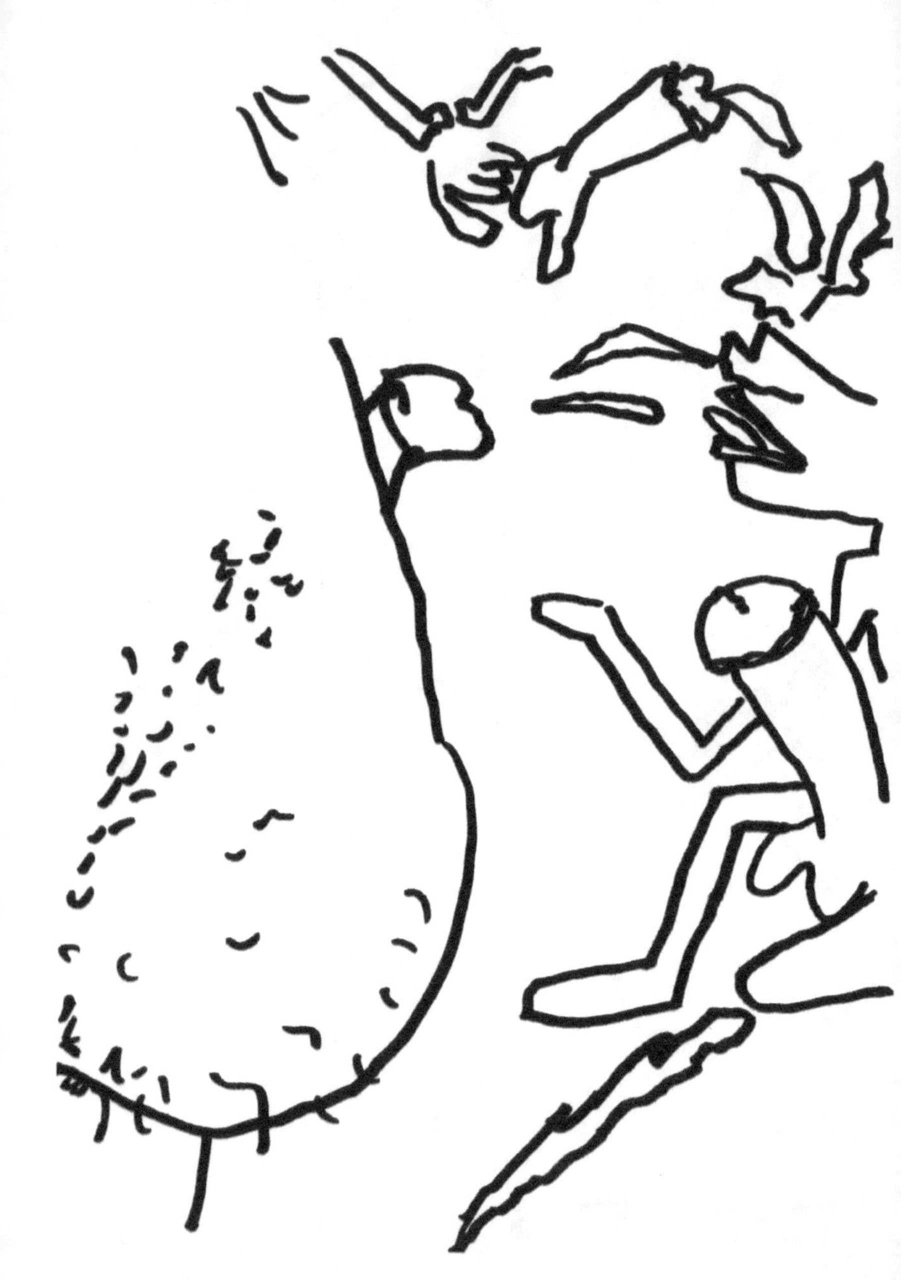

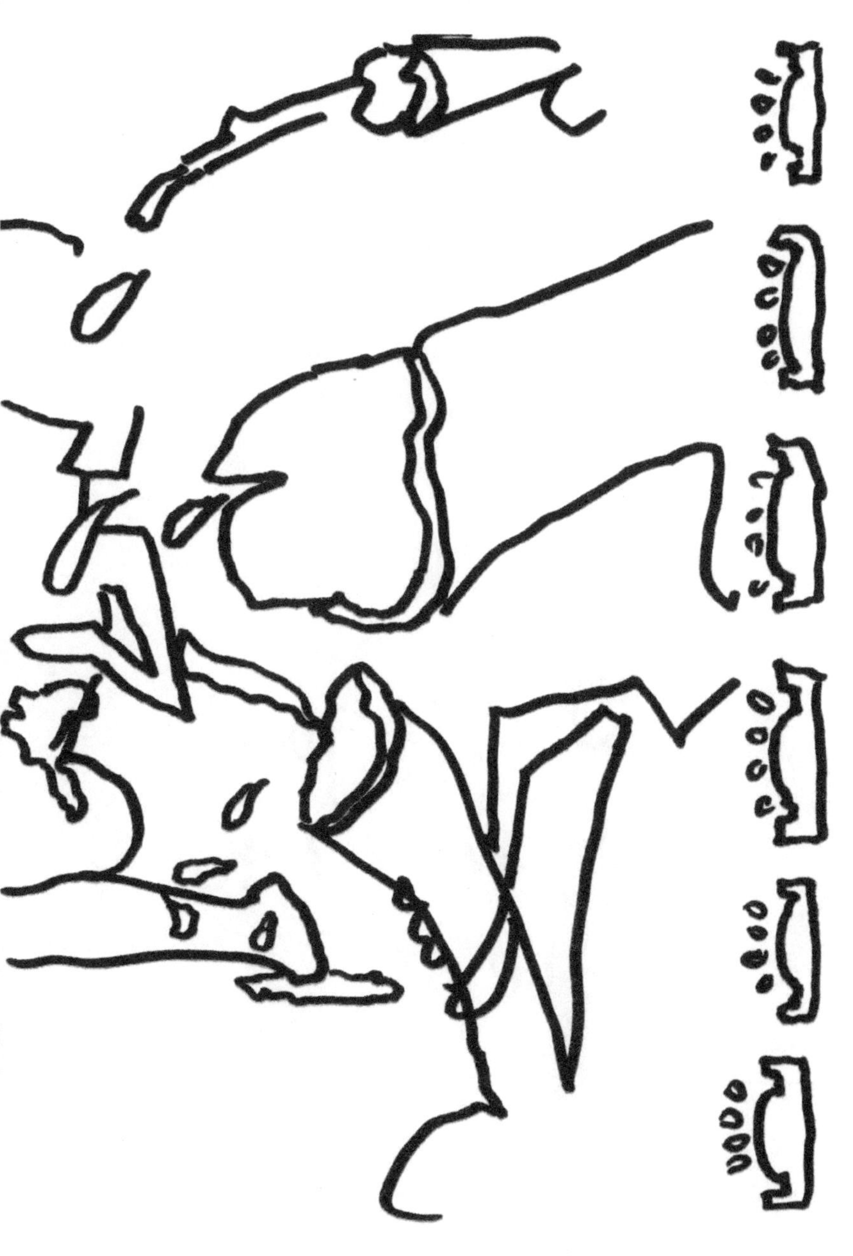

11, 12, 13,
14 YR OLD
J.D.P just
wanted to
die.

His
~~the~~ predilection
for same sex
attraction was
enough reason
for the child
to even devise
ways to do it.
                    end

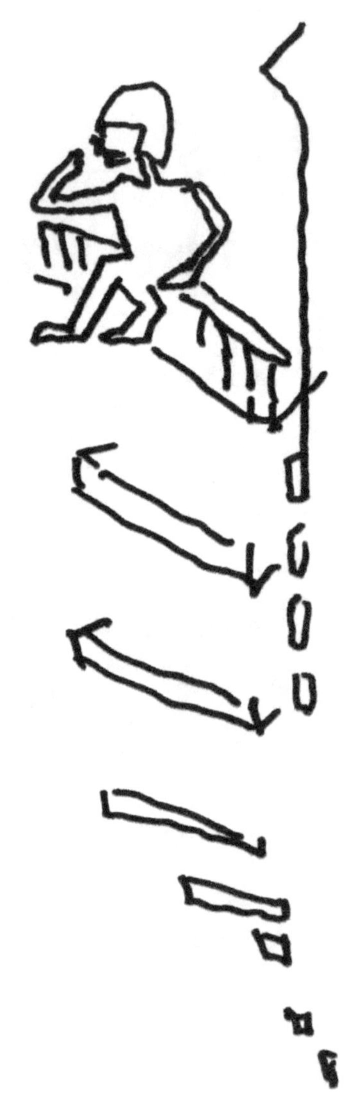

This way
was too
scary.

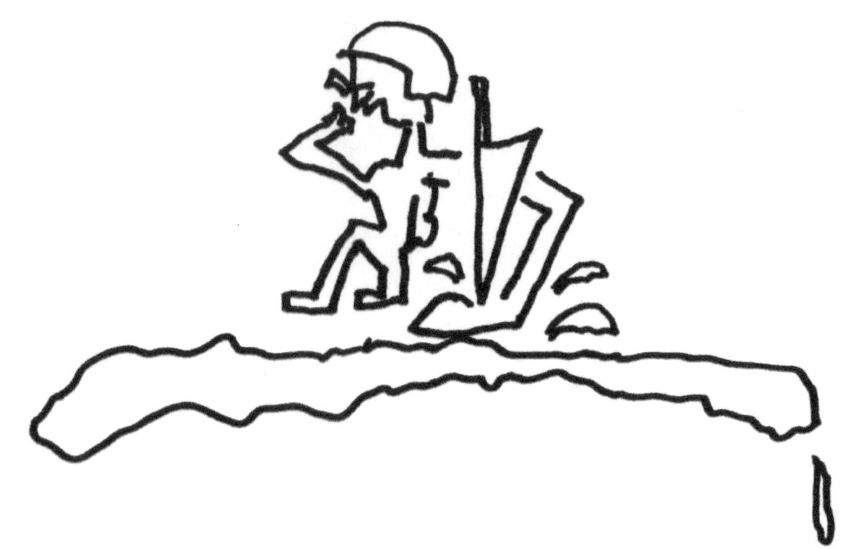

This way
was too
messy.

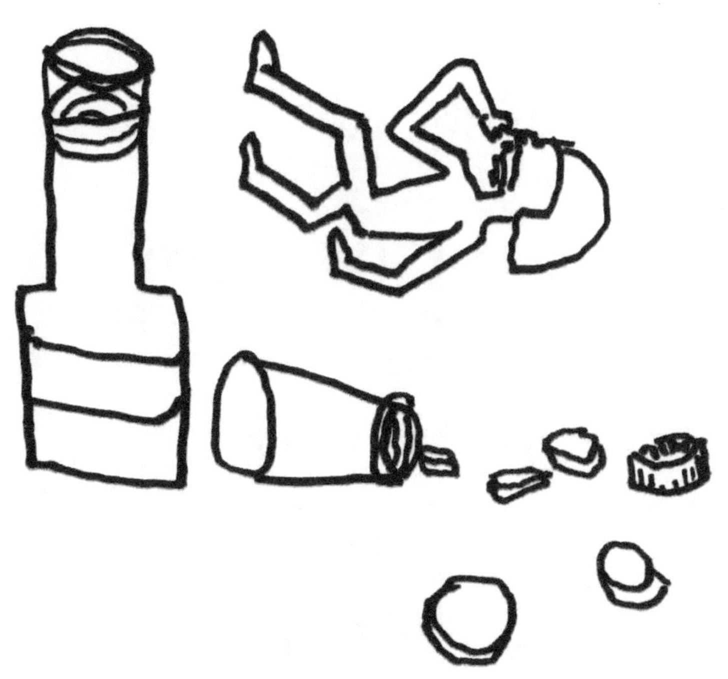

This way
was just
Right.

Judge not.

(Unless it's a gay
kid. Then
judge that
fucker Right
into the
ground.)

☆☆ MAIN Stage ☆☆

SATURDAY

Ulrichs

~~Gilgamesh~~

Enkidu ①

Patroclus

Hephaestian

Antinous

Extended!

Halford
Waters
Nassib   Lynde
Pete!!   Defert
          Lane...

David & Giovanni ③   special
Max & Rudy ①   guest
Ennis & Jack ③   stars

Balwdin   Rock   Orville
Wilde   James   Elton
Williams   Sal   Freddie!

ORTON

I WILL Love myself as I was
created
I will Love myself as I was
created
Love mysel
Love m
Love
Lore
Love myself
Love m

I will Love myself as I was
created.
I will love myself as I was
created

J.O.O.P SENT HIS

Young Ward
off to his
mission and
paid for his
tomb when
later he was
killed.

ALSO J.O.P.:

Let us
celebRate
the day
whem we
Recognize
ouR sameness
oveR all,
and the Real
Laws of Love,
win.
Let us Cuddle.